DEATH OF A DUCHESS

Detective Chief Inspector Cameron MacLeod is used to finding burglars and thieves, but when the body of a tramp is washed up on the beach he heads the investigation into her death. His curiosity and determination in solving the case lead to surprising results and dangerous situations. But can he intercept the murderer before another life is lost?

LYNN NIXON

DEATH OF A DUCHESS

Complete and Unabridged

LINFORD
Leicester

First published in Great Britain in 1997

First Linford Edition
published 2001

British Library CIP Data

Nixon, Lynn
Death of a duchess.—Large print ed.—
Linford mystery library
1. Detective and mystery stories
2. Large type books
I. Title
823.9'14 [F]

ISBN 0–7089–4594–5

Published by
F. A. Thorpe (Publishing)
Anstey, Leicestershire

Set by Words & Graphics Ltd.
Anstey, Leicestershire
Printed and bound in Great Britain by
T. J. International Ltd., Padstow, Cornwall

This book is printed on acid-free paper

1

'Mary,' a soft voice drifted from the black car parked at the pick-up point at Glasgow Central Railway Station. It was barely audible over the noises of the railway station.

A tramp leaning on the passenger guard rail looked up. She was dressed in the style of tramps, neither male nor female, the only indication of sex was the ubiquitous headscarf favoured by the female of the class.

'You've come then.' She smiled, showing less than well cared for teeth. She approached the car and got into the passenger seat, little knowing that this car ride would be her last.

It was late, few people were around to see this unusual event, a tramp sitting in the passenger seat of a car, as it slid quietly out of the railway station into the dark streets of Glasgow.

* * *

The tide was going out in a rush; wood, refuse and discarded waste bobbed and swirled in the fast water. Amongst the flotsam rolled a body. A woman, her glassy eyes stared unseeing upwards to dawn light. Her hair waved in the current.

Suddenly the body was struck a glancing blow by a passing fishing boat, the crew unaware of the grisly contact and she became almost animated, arms and legs undulating in the flow and she was nudged towards the shore.

Down on the shoreline were four boys, unusually for teenagers they were up early, but they had a good reason today. They were looking for whatever the tide had cast up during the night. They had to get the best pickings — there was a raft race later in the day and they needed to make a solid and watertight craft quickly.

Like a swarm of bees, they jumped and shrieked with all the energy of youth. They were shouting to each other at each 'find'. A piece of wood misshapen by the wind and tide was a treasure.

They were on their mid-term holiday and intended to make the most of it. It was a foolish bet made the day before to their friends that caused the early walk on the shore. Their parents would be in nervous shock when they found their beds empty: it was not natural for these boys to be up and about without being shouted at least five times. Today their parents' shock would be compounded by them being called to the police station.

One boy saw a battered suitcase bobbing and drifting towards the blue buoy out to the side of the Clyde. He ran on to the old slipway and jumped into the shallow water, taking care not to go too far.

He knew that the shelf was not far out and he did not want to get into deep water — he was a reasonable swimmer but the water was too cold for comfort.

He stretched out as far as he could, his black trainers were wet but he knew he could hide them from his parents — a whole outfit of clothing was another matter.

He poked the suitcase and managed to

drag it towards him, his friends were more of a hindrance than a help. One threw stones and nearly sunk the suitcase, he gave a cry of warning and told him to stop. With difficulty he got the suitcase to land.

His imagination told him that this was filled with money, thrown overboard from some passing ship by an International spy ring to be picked up later. His common sense told him otherwise: he knew it was a discarded piece of trash, probably thrown into the Clyde by careless incomers from Kilmun.

They did their gardening in the spring and threw the waste into the Clyde, when the tide went out a ribbon of rubbish could be seen floating towards the open sea. Sometimes even chairs and other small items of furniture were mixed amongst the refuse.

The boys dragged the suitcase to land. They decided that it would be better to open it at the old changing rooms away from prying eyes.

The case was heavy with salt water, as they dragged it into the first changing room. As they were examining the lock they saw a bundle of rags, or so they thought.

The leader decided to investigate the rags whilst his companions were struggling with the case. He pulled at an old coat and stood stock still. He wanted to run but his muscles were frozen.

He saw the body of a woman; her hair was matted, lying over her face. The blue tinge of her skin was wax-like. Her eyes were open — glazed and staring. He knew she was dead, he could not say anything.

He was not frightened, he was too shocked to feel anything. The other boys, perplexed, moved to stand behind him, looking over his shoulder, then one spoke.

'Is she dead?'

The spell of silence was broken, all thoughts of the suitcase forgotten, they turned as one and ran as fast as they could up towards the parade. They were looking for help and could see no one. The ferries had gone, no one would appear for at least another half hour.

Gasping for breath, they ran into the police station. They rang the bell.

A constable appeared and saw the hallway full of wet sweating babbling boys. He knew them by sight, and attempted to calm them down. All he could understand was 'Body', 'Dead', 'Shore', 'Parade'.

At the commotion the sergeant appeared with a mug of tea in his hand. He looked at the boys, their faces wide-eyed in shock. He had heard their gabbling and put his tea down. He said, 'Right, into the van, show me what has got you into this state.'

★ ★ ★

Detective Chief Inspector Cameron MacLeod was turning over for five minutes' lie in before he got out of bed. He always set the alarm a few minutes early because he enjoyed a couple of minutes to properly wake up before getting out of bed — he was not one of these people who awoke and leapt out of bed at the first ring of the alarm. The shrill noise of the telephone startled him, he became fully alert.

The telephone was at his wife's side of the bed, but he did not stretch over her to get it. Morag answered the phone and said 'Yes.' She never gave her name or telephone number which irritated Cameron at times.

He did not like answering the telephone in his own house, he said he had enough of it during the day without having to answer it at home. In reality he had two teenage daughters, Nicola and Jacqueline, and he felt that he was an answering service for them. It was fortunate indeed if he was called out for duty and the house telephone was not engaged.

Morag handed the phone to her husband and said, 'It's for you.' She then snuggled down to get a few minutes more rest.

'Okay, preserve the scene and I'll be there as soon as I can.' He turned to Morag, 'A body has been found at Dunoon.'

Morag looked at him, sighed and got out of bed. Although Dunoon was only over the water from their home in

7

Greenock, in fact they could see Dunoon from their window and she knew he would be too preoccupied to come home.

The last ferry was late in the evening but she knew her husband, he would work until he missed the last one or the first for that matter. He would need at least an overnight bag, perhaps a couple of shirts, underwear, socks and shaving kit. While Cameron was getting dressed she packed a small case for him.

Cameron was already working out in his mind what he would need, he knew he didn't have to hurry before the tide came back in, but he should get to the scene as soon as possible.

Morag handed Cameron his case as he left the house, she kissed him on the cheek, 'Give me a ring when you can, tell me when you are likely to be home, I'll ban the girls from the telephone after eight.'

He grunted, totally preoccupied, took the holdall and picked up his briefcase. He opened his jacket and checked he had his pens, wallet, and warrant card. This was his ritual on leaving the house, unfortunately this did not include his house keys and often Morag was awakened in the wee small hours to let him in.

MacLeod caught the eight o'clock ferry and was in the police station by eight thirty-five. He was greeted by Sergeant Gillespie.

'Morning sir, I hope the crossing was okay.'

MacLeod nodded and said, 'Fine. Have you set up the incident room?'

'Yes, we have set it up in the conference room on the first floor. BT have been called in to install extra telephones.'

'Right then, tell me about it while we go to the scene.'

Sergeant Gillespie and Detective Chief Inspector MacLeod got into the police van and drove to the scene. Sergeant Gillespie did all the talking. 'The body was found by some local boys. They have been collected by their parents now, and have been seen by the doctor as they were in shock — the local police surgeon is Doctor Lamont, but she has gone to a conference in London, so we got the police surgeon over from Greenock, Doctor Alan Wood, I think you know him.'

Without waiting for an answer he went on, 'He declared life extinct at seven forty-five, we had already rung you by then because I think it's a murder.' Gillespie did not elaborate. 'I've left the Fiscal to you.'

MacLeod needed no explanation, he knew the Procurators Fiscal of old, and hoped he did not want to take too personal an interest in the case. Telling the Fiscal too early in a case, although prescribed by law, could be a drawback.

'Doctor Wood said that he could not be sure of the cause of death. He usually can tell at a glance, as he has been in the business for many years and his first assessment is normally correct, but he thinks she has been stabbed and bled to death before she went into the water. The tide will not be in for some time yet so we left the body where it is, he wanted you to see it.'

Just then they arrived at the shore. The

10

area had been cordoned off and Constable MacDonald noted the time and route the two officers took to the scene.

Doctor Wood was at the cordon smoking a dark cheroot. He knew the effects of smoking well, as many a post-mortem showed blackened lungs, in fact he had a museum of 'interesting' lungs.

The cadavers did not necessarily have to have died from a smoking-related illness for him to acquire the organs for further research. Somehow the effects of his smoking on his own body did not occur to him. Everyone, especially doctors, believe they are immortal.

He was making notes in a tatty old notebook, and for all the world looked like a shabby reporter in his old well-worn mackintosh. He was wearing a pair of black wellies and was sitting on a shooting stick. He was a capable and competent pathologist, but had given up sartorial elegance for comfort many years ago. He had spent too much time examining bodies in the most uncomfortable places to worry what anyone thought of his appearance. The police paid him for his work, not his clothes.

He looked up as MacLeod approached, 'I won't know the cause of death until after the post-mortem, but she died before she went into the water, stab wound I should think, I can't tell you what kind of blade, so don't ask.'

They went down to the old changing rooms and MacLeod saw the body of a female. She was lying on her back with her eyes closed, her skin was pallid and blue, there was a small cut on her left cheek which was white against her skin. Her mouth was open but no water dribbled from it.

Her face was peaceful and calm which was not her normal expression in life. She was dressed in shabby clothes and her hands were clenched. Reddish brown stains were visible on the front of her coat, and he could see sharp tears, unlike the other frayed edges due to wear and tear.

She appeared to be a woman of late middle age, her skin was toughened and weather-beaten, from the state of her clothing MacLeod assessed, correctly, she had been living rough. She was wearing a pair of men's boots, the left one he could see at a glance was a different shade and make to the right.

Her fists were clenched, he could not see her fingernails but knew by instinct that they were dirty. Although this woman had been in the sea, it could not erase the grime embedded in her skin. He did not touch the body, she was an interesting problem at the moment, as he discovered more about her she would become a human being, but for now she could have been any piece of flotsam thrown up on the shore.

Doctor Wood turned to MacLeod and said, 'Look at this,' he pointed to the cadaver's hands, 'No defensive wounds. If she was conscious when she was stabbed there should be wounds on the hands. Anyone suffering an attack like that always put up their hands to ward off the attack. Her hands are intact.'

Doctor Wood prodded a stick at the right hand and held it up for inspection, 'She must have been unconscious before she was stabbed. I'll have to find out why, in fact some of the wounds could have been after death. I just don't know.'

MacLeod bent down and examined the grimy hands more closely, he did not like the fact of death and found the mechanics somewhat nauseating.

He thought privately that this was becoming 'curiouser and curiouser'; why anyone should take the trouble to make this woman unconscious *before* stabbing her was interesting. He looked at the coat, it was ripped and torn in an almost frenzied attack. A calculated killer rendered the body unconscious and thus caused the death but then the frenzied attack? Perhaps two people involved, or perhaps not.

MacLeod shook his head, and stopped himself jumping to any more conclusions. He accompanied Doctor Wood to the parade and told Constable MacDonald to have the body removed.

Arrangements to move the body had been made by Sergeant Gillespie and the body wagon was waiting at the side of the road. Two bored men from the local undertakers were leaning against the closed back door of the hearse, it was a black Mercedes: in death she would ride in better style than in life.

Doctor Wood had asked that they should take the body to the Inverclyde Hospital in Gourock. He said to MacLeod as they parted company, 'I want the body at my laboratory, I know it may inconvenience the Fiscal but I need it there, I'm not happy to give any cause of death until I have conducted more tests, but you may tell the Fiscal it was murder. It may be by lethal weapon, it may not and until I am satisfied how it happened that's all I'm saying so don't nag me.'

At that he abruptly turned and got into his car and drove off.

Sergeant Gillespie approached MacLeod and said, 'The Scenes of Crime officer has already been here, he's taken the photographs. They should be ready in about an hour.'

MacLeod ordered that everything in the surrounding area should be collected and tagged, he did not have any hope that anything could be of value, a floating body rarely, if ever, carries anything of value to an investigation, the only clues he could hope for was from the clothing or forensic results. He noted a small suitcase near the body. Gillespie saw him looking at the suitcase.

'The boys told me that they had dragged it from the sea, I don't think it is of any value.'

MacLeod grunted and said, 'Take it anyway.'

As he stood up MacLeod glanced out to sea towards Greenock, he saw the red and white western ferry pulling away from the jetty. He wondered who the mystery woman was, he didn't know — yet — but he would. Of that he was certain.

2

Detective Superintendent Alisdair Hamilton had just arrived at his office. He was contemplating his well organised day before him with some pleasure. He had a hot cup of coffee on the mahogany desk before him, when the telephone rang, 'Detective Superintendent Hamilton.'

He felt a cloud settle over his head when he heard the voice of MacLeod. MacLeod never rang him unless it was important and he had learned that he rarely, if ever engaged in general pleasantries. He had also learned that MacLeod always caused havoc with the long-term costings and statistics of the department. His good mood began to dissipate.

'A body has been found in Dunoon and the circumstances are suspicious, I want extra staff and authorisation for overtime.'

'Has the cause of death been confirmed?'

MacLeod sighed inwardly, his thoughts were unrepeatable, if it hadn't been confirmed he would hardly be ringing up now would he, 'Not officially, but it looks like a stabbing. I'll know the result in about an hour or so.'

'I don't work on mere suspicion, I'll have to look at it and make a decision later.'

Hamilton hated making decisions on the spot, he needed to consider his options before he could bring himself to give an opinion.

'Ring me back when you have the results of the PM and I'll see what I can do.'

'I think we should set up a small squad now, time at the beginning of an enquiry is invaluable.'

Hamilton interrupted, he wouldn't be pushed into a hasty decision.

'I don't think or work like that, I need to have some facts, not your instincts, I distrust instinct.'

'The Fiscal hasn't been told yet, I will see him and tell him what you have said.' MacLeod said this in a matter of fact tone but he got his point over.

Hamilton knew then that he was about to be circumvented, the Procurators Fiscal in Scotland is the man responsible for all criminal matters and the police act as his agent. Whatever the Fiscal says, goes.

If he rang the Fiscal he would be questioned and he knew he would not be able to answer and Hamilton loathed appearing less than perfect. He did not have the operational experience to quite feel confident in a situation such as this. He enjoyed the power of his job but not the responsibility.

It was only officers such as MacLeod who could detect his uncertainty and consciously, or unconsciously, use it to their advantage.

Hamilton then made a decision, which was one of self-preservation rather than one of common sense. He may say that he mistrusted instinct but was human enough to sometimes follow his inner voices. He had a feeling that this case could have a serious effect on his future.

Hamilton had taken the new system of management to heart. Government had decreed that those who spend the public purse should be responsible for it. In the past, the police, as with all in the public domain, concentrated solely on the task in hand, they rarely, if ever had to account in cash terms for their actions.

Hamilton had never been what is termed a Street Copper, the streets held no charm for him. As a man of thirty-four he was one of the youngest in the country to reach the rank of superintendent but had to perform some operational work to further his career.

The Criminal Investigation Department was his chosen field to gain the operational mark on his record. He thought that being in uniform held greater pitfalls for a budding very senior officer, than the CID. How wrong he was.

His decision was based on his observations in the force. He knew that most CID officers were experienced enough to carry him, whereas in the uniform branch a mistake made by an inexperienced junior officer could cause his career to come to a sudden and premature halt.

Whatever was said about Hamilton's

attributes or otherwise, being a fool was not one of them, he knew his limitations. In his considered opinion the operational requirement was a complete waste of time for him — after all he was going to be a Chief Constable one day. However he needed this period recorded on his CV or he would not get to that exalted rank.

'Okay, ring the Fiscal and I will come over to Dunoon and take charge of the case. I will get the overtime and men needed, once you tell me what is required. I bow to your experience, but don't gild the lily, we haven't got a bottomless pit for cash. Get an office ready for me at the incident room.'

MacLeod put the phone down, he was bemused, he could not understand why Hamilton had decided to take charge of the case. He had never done it before and he gave no reason for doing it now.

In reality Hamilton was always in charge of serious cases, but in the past he had been in charge from his office. He had not come out on to the streets and physically been present, he tended to get reports and think about them, from a distance he could be objective and criticise or interfere whenever it seemed appropriate.

As far as MacLeod was concerned finance was not his concern, but he placed more importance on the job in hand. Victims of crime were not able to understand that they could not have the service they needed because the money has run out, pain does not have a price.

'The detective superintendent is coming here, get an office for him, I'm off to see the Fiscal, I can't do much until the PM result is through. I have my mobile phone with me ring me as soon as you get the results. Ring my office, get Detective Inspector Reade over to the Inverclyde to attend the PM, then come here.'

MacLeod knew that Doctor Wood, an experienced pathologist, would not start the post-mortem until someone from the CID arrived. MacLeod did not like bodies and he used his privilege of rank to side step this task. He may be a hands-on detective, but attending postmortems was not one of his favourite tasks.

'DS Milton, Constable Morris and MacPherson are to come straight here to set up the incident room. Anyone else will have to be brought in when Hamilton makes the decision.'

'We've had the national press on the phone already, what do I say to them?'

MacLeod grinned and said, 'Tell them to ring the press officer, when the Superintendent arrives I'm sure he will be able to cope with the press. It will keep him busy if I'm not back.'

As he was walking to the door he stopped, 'Has the Wicked Witch of the West been on the phone?'

Helen MacDonald, the local reporter, had worked for the local paper for years but she did not fit the image of a female reporter, in fact she could be a farm hand. She was tall and strong, with short red hair. Her temper matched her hair but she was a good reporter, born and brought up in this area, only returning after her marriage to a local businessman.

Helen could have been a successful reporter on a national Daily, but she simply was happy in her work on the local paper. This was her first and only job, she had no aspirations to go anywhere else.

'Of course, three or four times, she was even at the locus almost as soon as we were, but we managed to persuade her to leave.'

Gillespie grinned and MacLeod refrained from asking how they managed that feat.

'Perhaps Detective Superintendent Hamilton should talk to her next time.'

MacLeod had a wicked sense of humour and chuckled at the vision of them conversing. It was a pity he would not be there. But he would bet on Helen rather than Hamilton coming out best from the encounter.

MacLeod left the police office and went to the Fiscal's office in George Street. Dunoon is a small town and he knew that the Fiscal would already know about the body.

He felt pleased with himself, it was only ten past nine but he felt that he had been working for hours, he enjoyed a good case.

Behind the screen was a middle-aged

lady who had kept herself in good shape, she was not skinny, she had never been that, but was pleasantly plump with greying hair, short and wavy, she wore a small amount of make up.

She looked up and saw MacLeod. 'How can I help . . . good grief it's Cameron, I wondered who was going to come over, I haven't seen you in years! Well this is a law abiding town and we hardly ever get anything like this. How's your wife? Are the children okay? They must be growing up.'

Just then a voice from the inner sanctum cried out.

'Maureen, for goodness' sake, let the man in, you will drown him with your words.'

Mrs Stewart straightened her shoulders and got up from her chair, she said in a formal manner, 'Sorry. Please follow me.'

MacLeod was amused, he had not said a word since he walked in, but as he was ushered into the Fiscal's office she whispered in his ear, 'Hope to see you later and catch up.'

Behind the desk Duncan Grey, the

Procurator Fiscal for the area of Dunoon was sitting, he was a tall man, slim in his youth, but his rugby playing days had left him with a distinctive nose and the beginnings of a cauliflower ear, he had played in the days before masking tape wrapped around the head to attempt to stop such disfigurement.

His eyes sparkled and was slow in speech, however anyone taking his slowness in speech as slowness in thought was sadly mistaken. He had a rapier-like intellect, woe betide any defendant or defence lawyer for that matter who underestimated him.

The desk was covered with papers, small and large piles, he did not have in and out trays, his habit was to put the papers he had finished with on the floor on the right side of his desk.

Mrs Stewart installed a small table to his left a couple of years ago when she felt the lifting was straining her back, and had told him to put the papers on the table or she would either consider suing him under the Health and Safety at Work legislation, or he could pick the papers up himself and put them on her desk. Duncan Grey was compliant, after all she had only to ask. He put the papers on the small desk.

On a desk at the side of the large desk was a computer. It was not switched on. MacLeod looked at this piece of technology and smiled. He and Duncan had spoken about computers in the past and he remembered how vehemently Duncan had said he would not have such a piece of devil's work in his office.

'Yes, it's a computer and, yes, I find it useful, so that is the end of the conversation. It's good to see you Cameron. It's a long time since we were relative rookies here years ago.'

He held out his hand and they shook hands like good friends who had not seen each other for many years.

'A pleasure, Fiscal, but it is a pity in such circumstances. Before we go on to business, I must ask, why when you became Fiscal did you stay in this office and not move down the corridor?'

'I like this office and after so many years as a depute I thought about the turmoil in moving and decided to stay where I was.'

MacLeod looked at Grey quizzically, 'It's Cameron you are talking to, could it be that you couldn't bear to be shoved into an office away from everything?'

Grey's laugh was a deep roar, 'The old Cameron, you will never change! You remember what we kept from the old man, but I'm the old man now, so none of your tricks.'

'Not much chance with you as Fiscal and my detective superintendent coming down to take charge of the case.'

Grey was suddenly serious, 'Why is he doing that, it's unusual, is this a high powered case?'

MacLeod shook his head, 'Hardly, the victim is a tramp.'

'There is no accounting for senior police officers' decisions, I've found to my utter bewilderment. Now to business, why did I find out about this murder from my receptionist when I came in and not from you?'

Grey was a total professional and never mixed friendship with business, no matter who he was talking to. Off duty he was a friend to be cherished, however on duty he was fair to all, and no one dared bring up friendship in his office especially when he was conducting business.

MacLeod described the body and the scene. 'I saw what I think are stab tears in the coat, we think she was thrown in, we haven't found the locus of the crime as yet.'

MacLeod paused, he was thinking that someone had to be very cheeky to drop a body in the water in this area, or he didn't know the area very well. He went on, 'I think it was this side of the water, when we get more men we will look for signs, maybe the locals will find it before us. I hope we find it before they do, the pathologist indicated that she bled considerably and it must be soaked in blood, but we need as much help as possible with this one. I don't want the area trampled.'

'Have you any idea who she was?' interrupted Grey.

'Unfortunately no, her clothing suggests she was living rough, she seemed familiar somehow. I don't know where or when but I feel I knew her from somewhere, perhaps she was living rough for some years. I can't seem to be able to remember, it may come to me.'

MacLeod paused, he was trying to put the name to a face with singular lack of success.

'Go on,' said Grey, 'or we will be here all day.' MacLeod shrugged his shoulders and continued.

'I was hoping that there will be some means of identification in her pockets, but nothing has been found as yet. As you know tramps don't carry driving licences and rarely are reported missing. The body and clothing are at the Inverclyde.'

Grey was a little put out that anyone had the audacity to ditch a body in his sphere of influence and then have it taken away without his knowledge. He was a little testy as he asked MacLeod, 'What is the body doing at the Inverclyde? Doctor Lamont is my police surgeon.'

'Doctor Lamont is at a conference in London and Doctor Wood pronounced life extinct. He is to do the PM and he wanted the body taken to his laboratory.'

Grey calmed down a little, his feathers had been ruffled and realised he was acting a little childishly but he had to tell MacLeod how he felt.

'You should have asked me first, I don't like the body being taken out of my jurisdiction without knowing about it.'

MacLeod smiled, Fiscals are always touchy about jurisdiction.

'You would have said yes, wouldn't you? I was saving you an early call.'

Grey burst out laughing, 'You remember me well, I can be a bit bad-tempered when I get woken up in the early hours, yes I would not have made any objection — eventually. Now Cameron I think I will take a look at the scene, I know the body has been moved, it's a pity, I would have liked to have seen it, but I suppose you were only thinking of me.'

MacLeod felt the faint stirrings of alarm, first the superintendent coming over to take personal charge, now the Fiscal was exercising his rights. It started off being such a good meaty problem, now it seemed as if everyone wanted to get in on the act.

'You know where the body was found, in the old changing rooms, all the items round the scene have been seized and taken to the police station, but I'm not too hopeful for any clues there. I will have photographs for you later, but, you are the boss, I've got a car outside, I'll take you there.'

Grey kept a straight face, he had no intention of going to the scene, he did need to show his authority at times. He knew MacLeod of old and this man needed some reminders who was in charge, the fact that he was going to go to the scene was enough to emphasise the point. He barely concealed his amusement at MacLeod's reaction.

'I think I may be a little too busy at the moment, if it is as you say I may come over to the police station later.'

He looked at his papers on his desk, hardly daring to gaze into his friend's eyes, he did not think he could disguise his mirth.

MacLeod's mobile phone rang, he answered and said, 'I'll be there in a couple of minutes, I think the Fiscal has finished with me.'

He nodded towards Grey who inclined his head with approval.

'Get on with it Cameron, but I will expect regular updates, every twenty-four hours is a minimum.'

MacLeod grimaced and left.

3

MacLeod returned to the police station, he estimated that he had about an hour before Hamilton arrived, he needed breathing space to collect his thoughts. He did not like being supervised, especially by Hamilton; it was not because he disliked the man, it was his age and lack of experience that irritated him. Unlike other graduate entries to the police service, Hamilton did seem to try to understand his problems and which MacLeod appreciated, but he felt that Hamilton was using his beloved CID and the only loyalty he had was to himself. In MacLeod's book that was the worst crime of all.

He saw Sergeant Gillespie in the front office and he said, 'Detective Inspector Reade rang, the pathologist said that she died of a stab wound to the heart.'

Gillespie consulted the scribbled notes he had taken.

'Doctor Wood is sure that a thin blade was used, a very sharp knife, there are at least ten wounds on the body, some were inflicted after death. There is a deeper knife wound at the base of the neck, the carotid artery had been cut but the direct cause of death was one deep wound directly in the heart. She will have bled considerably, both the locus and the killer must have been saturated in blood.'

He stopped, MacLeod knew that he would be unlikely to get any more from the sergeant. He was a methodical man and would have made accurate notes, he took the notes from him. MacLeod asked if his staff had arrived.

'Yes sir, they are in the conference room, they have been busy setting up the incident room. I had put an office for you but I have changed it for the superintendent, I don't know if you want to work in the same office or in the main incident room. We don't have another, sorry about that. John Milton is up there now.'

MacLeod considered the point. Much as he was tempted to work in the main incident room, he knew it would be off-putting for both himself and his staff, and so he reluctantly decided to work in the same office as Hamilton.

MacLeod hoped not to be in the office too much, he worked as hard, if not harder than his staff, they knew that and they never complained about working excess hours, more often than not they did not get paid for it.

MacLeod was not a 'political' police officer, he got on with his job and if something needed to be said, he said it. It did not make him popular with either his supervisors or in some cases, his subordinates. However, he could be devious when necessary but he disliked any underhand methods on his own or any one else's part. It did not fit in with his style of policing. He liked to call a spade a spade, but in most cases it was a bloody shovel.

MacLeod was trying to figure out what motive Hamilton had in wanting to physically take charge of the operation. He shrugged his thoughts away from Hamilton, if a problem was insoluble at the moment he knew he would get the answer sometime. Maybe it would be in a few days, weeks or even months, the answer would arrive when he least expected it, but it would come.

MacLeod walked into the incident room and saw Detective Constable Morris busy sorting out incident log, setting up the computers and generally getting the office organised. He was telling the BT engineers where the telephones were to be placed, and the fax machine.

Detective Constable MacPherson was setting out the incident boards. A Polaroid photograph of the deceased was in the centre of the larger. A better and bigger photograph would be obtained from the cadaver in the mortuary, perhaps those from the scene would arrive soon.

A map of the surrounding area dominated the room.

MacPherson said, 'I've got the tide tables, boss. She could have been dumped anywhere around this area.'

He indicated the whole of the upper

part of the map including Holy Loch and Gareloch.

MacLeod thought, 'Good lad, shows he is thinking, must keep an eye on him, he could make a very good Sergeant', but said, 'Seems that we are going to have our work cut out.'

'Morning, sir, how was the Fiscal? Happy I hope.' Sergeant Milton appeared from the adjoining office.

'As happy as ever, where's my office?'

MacLeod looked at his staff. Detective Sergeant John Milton and he were of an age, they had worked together as detectives in the City, each had a healthy respect for the other's abilities. Once MacLeod had been promoted to detective inspector he had ensured that Milton had been posted to him as his 'bag-carrier'.

In reality he wanted Milton with him, he once had a young officer as his side-kick and found the age gap disconcerting. He liked to be with a man he could trust, who had been brought up in the same way as himself.

Morris and MacPherson were as different as chalk and cheese. Morris was a slim, delicate looking young man, he wore glasses and always had a puzzled look on his face, he blushed easily and had got used to being the object of derision by the 'macho' men of the force.

His partner MacPherson was completely the opposite, he was big and powerfully built, he was not a person that anyone would willingly cross, he had a menacing air about him, he knew it and tried hard not to frighten the punters but was unable to do anything about it.

Morris and MacPherson worked well, they enjoyed each other's company and respected each other's strengths and weaknesses.

Detective Inspector Reade arrived, he was smart, as always, his hair was immaculate, and he immediately came to the point.

'The pathologist will send his report as soon as it is typed. I believe that I gave the salient points to Gillespie. Did he give you the message?'

MacLeod said, 'Yes, anything else I should know?'

'Yes, as he could not find any defensive

cuts on the hand, he is certain that she was unconscious when she was stabbed, he is sending blood and the stomach contents to the lab for analysis. He doesn't think she was in the water above twelve hours. I brought the clothing and Morris will be exhibits officer.'

He shouted into the incident room, 'Morris, once the DCI has finished with the items, take them to forensic, we don't want the clothing to get mildewed.'

Reade turned to MacLeod, 'Her liver was enlarged, she only had about six months to live. She was an alcoholic, perhaps three or four bottles of Red Biddy a day.'

Reade did not need to explain the reference to this sort of strong wine, it was cheap and readily available.

He went on, 'There was a small piece of paper in her pocket bearing these numbers, five-six-seven-two.'

He showed MacLeod a plastic bag with a piece of paper, just visible were the numbers.

'I have had her fingerprints taken and they have been sent to SCRO, she may have a record, if so we can find out who she is.'

Detective Inspector Reade stopped. He was usually more friendly, but he felt a little put out, the smell of the mortuary with formaldehyde, ether and the post-mortem itself disturbed him. He was not squeamish but he hated to see the first cut, up to then he saw a human being, after the first cut it was a piece of meat and he was fine.

MacLeod did not pry into the reasons why Reade was so formal, he knew that post-mortem examinations usually caused a reaction to even the most blasé.

This team had worked together for some four years before he joined it two years ago and he used both their strengths and weaknesses to both his and the team's advantage.

MacLeod gathered the team together in the incident room. 'Time to start.'

He waited until everyone had settled down with a cup of coffee in their hands and began.

'Detective Sergeant Milton,' MacLeod was always formal at a briefing, 'get

Sergeant Gillespie here and find out how many officers he can release to do the usual house to house enquiries. I want Alexandra Parade and Queens Street done as soon as possible. The shop at Kirn opens at 7 a.m. so they may have seen something, you work out the usual questions. I would like this finished today, we will get the commuters tomorrow when they head for the ferries, maybe someone saw something, but I won't hold my breath.'

MacLeod looked at the map on the wall and continued, 'Talk to the coast guard they may give us a clue to exactly where she may have been dumped into the water.'

'Constable Morris, as you like computers, you will be the support and production officer, but get the forensic items to the labs now, there isn't much to do yet and I'm sure you will be able to catch up when you get back. I want you, Constable MacPherson, to visit the lads who found the body, don't frighten them.'

Morris gave no sign of displeasure at the last remark, he had many a remark like that throughout his career. He merely sighed.

'And please take a policewoman with you, I'm sure there is one here at Dunoon. She may not be on duty but Sergeant Gillespie will get her for you, the overtime is authorised, tell him to record it to this case.'

MacLeod thought for a few seconds and then went on, 'I think that is all we can do at the moment, except for this number, it could be a telephone number. When we find out who she is then we will have more of a chance, Morris when you get back from forensic, find out where this number comes from, check the whole area including Glasgow, that should keep you busy.'

MacLeod went on, 'Have I missed anything?'

MacLeod waited for any further suggestions from the team, nothing was forthcoming.

'Come with me Peter,' he and Reade went into the small office, leaving the rest of the team to get on with their allocated jobs.

In the office he told Reade that Detective Superintendent Hamilton would arrive imminently to take personal charge of the case, Reade's eyebrows raised but he said nothing.

'We will probably need two more men when we find out who this woman is, once the coast guard work out the tides we will need more men to search the shore line, hopefully we'll find the locus then. What's your gut reaction?'

Reade considered for a moment, 'She's a down and out, I think Hamilton will try to close this down as soon as he can. No one gives a damn about them.'

MacLeod interrupted, 'Maybe they don't but I do so what's your estimate of our chances of success?'

'Well, she's been murdered, we don't know where it happened, we don't know who she is, there's no motive. We don't have much of a chance, but we've solved murders with much less before, so I think we should go for it, stuff the overtime.'

'Good, she was someone's daughter once, I need your support before Hamilton arrives.'

44

4

MacLeod was thinking, he was trying to imagine living on the streets. He had known of a number of deaths of tramps, but this was different. Most tramps were killed by their peer group, for a drink, for a special place where they slept, for any number of reasons, but he had never come across a tramp being thrown into the river in an attempt to conceal the body.

There was no reason with tramps. They were the flotsam of society, no one cared, not even enough to hide a body. This was different and the difference excited him at one level of his consciousness, he wouldn't admit it, but police work was becoming too routine for him, nothing appeared new, there were no more surprises. This was a surprise and he revelled in the challenge.

Detective Sergeant John Milton came into the room, he saw the look on

MacLeod's face, 'What's up, boss?'

'I was wondering how anyone ends up on the streets.'

'That's easy, drink, drugs and mental illness or a combination of all three.'

MacLeod sighed and said, 'You are always so literal, John, everything is black and white with you, no shades of grey. At least I can rely on you for an answer, even if it isn't the one I want to hear.'

'It isn't good to dwell on something you can't do anything about, now what's really the matter?'

'This is different. Tramps are killed for many reasons, I've known them murdered by other down and outs for a drink, their place to sleep, or by normal thugs out for a night of fun and using them as their punch bags, I even knew one died when his sleeping bag was set on fire but not like this.'

'Come on, tell me what's so different here.'

MacLeod considered his reply and said, 'This seems like a crime of passion, she was stabbed many times after being rendered unconscious, and the body was thrown into the Clyde. Have you looked at her, how could she raise anyone's passion?'

Milton was about to reply when Detective Superintendent Hamilton burst through the door.

'That woman should have a gag, I'm drained.'

MacLeod stifled a smile. Hamilton had met Helen MacDonald with a vengeance. 'I knew you would be able to cope, after all you have done the course.'

'Okay, how far have we got and when are we going to wrap this one up?'

MacLeod's hackles rose but he controlled himself and said through gritted teeth, 'We have just started and I can't tell you when we are going to finish.'

'I hope it isn't too long, the budget won't take a prolonged enquiry. I told the assistant chief constable we were coming in under budget and I will make sure we do.'

Fortunately for the relationship between the two men Detective Inspector Reade came into the room. He produced a map and threw it on MacLeod's desk, they gathered round.

'We've got the men to search, the coast guards have indicated on the map the area where she could have been dumped in the water, it's a big shore and it could take some time.'

Hamilton looked at the map with horror, he said with rising panic, 'This could take some time and think of the manpower we are using, I think we can only search for eight hours and then call a halt, she was only a tramp and we shouldn't take too much time over this.'

MacLeod ignored the last remark and said, 'Have we examined the contents of the case? It may narrow the area a bit.'

He looked at Hamilton, this man was capable of pulling the plug at any time and he needed the locus to get any chance of a detection.

Detective Sergeant Milton brought the case into the room, it was still damp and it was unlocked, the label attached to the handle sagged. He opened the case, it was full of old papers, envelopes were torn like confetti.

'Well, we will have to do our jigsaws

now,' MacLeod said to the assembled personnel. They spent the next half hour carefully reconstructing the envelopes.

MacLeod could not have delegated the task to anyone else, Hamilton had promised more men but they had not arrived as yet. MacLeod wanted to prove a point to his boss. A lesson Hamilton learned, but never admitted it to anyone but himself.

At last an address, Mr and Mrs Lund, 18 High Street, Kilmun. MacLeod said to Reade, 'Start the search at Ardentinny, towards Kilmun, west of the hotel. If Milton and I get a better location I will contact you.'

MacLeod and Milton left the office, Hamilton watched them leave. He said to Reade, 'Is he always like this, a bit testy and he doesn't say much?'

'No sir, sometimes he can be quite chatty, but we all know our jobs he doesn't have to give detailed instructions.'

Reade had no desire to continue the conversation, he had too much respect for MacLeod and a healthy respect for his own career to make an enemy of this man. 'When did you say the reinforcements would be arriving?'

'I sent for two female detectives, as she was a woman I thought a couple of women would be better.'

Reade looked at Hamilton with horror, 'Females, he won't like that,' and shook his head.

'What do you mean, women have reached the highest ranks in the police service, they are as good as, if not better in some cases then men.'

'I didn't say he didn't have any respect for women, he just doesn't like working with them, he says he doesn't understand them, they think differently, anyway sir, you chose two women because the body is female, not because of their work, that's sexist.'

Hamilton bristled, 'I didn't mean that I chose them because they are female, I mean . . . well, you know what I mean.'

He spluttered to silence. He thought of his reaction and privately admitted he may have got this one wrong, he would have to watch himself, any sign of sexism or racism and he could say goodbye to his further career.

It was fortunate that MacLeod did not hear this conversation, he had no axe to grind where females were concerned, what he objected to was the way some of the women expected to be treated better than the men, in his team everyone was equal, they all got the rough end of his tongue when necessary, despite having an all female household, he still could not cope with tearful women. It disturbed him and he felt out of control.

5

MacLeod and Milton approached a neat cottage on the shore line of Kilmun, it was white painted and the windows were clean and tidy.

MacLeod always assessed the interior of a house by the state of the windows, a neat clean window, the house would be a home, dirty untidy windows, the house would be a hovel, and he would not accept a cup of tea if offered.

Only once was he wrong, he walked into a council house happily expecting a home and he was met with a pungent smell of rotting potato peelings carelessly discarded on the grimy floor of the kitchen.

The occupants did not notice the smell, they were used to it, however he had to leave with streaming eyes and conduct his enquiry on the doorstep.

Milton rapped the door and it was opened by a tall grey haired woman in her late seventies.

'Yes, what can I do for you?' she said, as she wiped her hands on her apron.

'Mrs Lund, I am Detective Sergeant Milton, this is Detective Chief Inspector MacLeod, can we come in?'

She looked concerned and MacLeod quickly spoke to her, 'There's no trouble we are making enquiries and perhaps you could help us.'

'Come in, it's baking day and I've made some scones, would you like some?'

She put her hand on Milton's arm, 'You look as though you need feeding, I'll put the kettle on.'

Milton and MacLeod looked at each other, they smiled and shrugged their shoulders in unison, anyone who thought Milton needed feeding was either blind or possessed of an overdeveloped maternal instinct. Fortunately it was the latter in Mrs Lund's case.

They followed her into the small but very neat living room, there was a table in the corner and Mrs Lund indicated that they should sit.

'Now don't say anything until we have the tea on the table.'

She bustled out to the small kitchen and came back with a tray with china cups and a huge pot of tea, she went back to the kitchen and brought out scones, bread and butter, sugar, milk and cream. In fact she produced a high tea that MacLeod had not seen since the days he visited his grandmother.

They had not spoken a word, in fact they had not been able to get a word in edgeways. Mrs Lund conducted a monologue and soon they knew that she had recently been widowed, her children rarely visited, she got on very well with her good neighbours, the funeral was conducted with great taste and style by the local undertaker.

She was not from these parts but they had retired some years earlier, her husband had died suddenly from a heart attack just before their fiftieth wedding anniversary.

'Now, how can I help you?' she said at last when she sat down with them.

MacLeod and Milton looked at each

other, they were wilting at this energetic lady.

'Do you recognise this?' Milton showed her the envelope they had carefully pieced together, she took out a pair of half moon glasses, put them on and read the envelope.

'Oh! yes, I was clearing out the bedroom and sorted out all the old papers, where on earth did you get it?'

'In an old suitcase found in Dunoon.'

She thought for a moment, 'Dear me. I remember now, I took as much as I could to the skip in Dunoon, you know behind the Bowling Club at Bogleha. When I got home I found this old suitcase in the back of the car. Well I wasn't going to make another trip so I threw it away.'

'When exactly did you throw it away?' enquired MacLeod.

'I told you, last night about eight o'clock, don't you listen young man?'

MacLeod sighed, it was his grand-mother talking to him again, he was fifteen years old and she was lecturing him, 'You must listen or you will never know anything, young man.' He could hear her now.

Milton saw the look of resignation on MacLeod's face, he was, unusually, being intimidated by this formidable lady and took over the gentle questioning.

'Where did you throw it away?'

'I hope I'm not going to get into any trouble for this.'

Milton feigned surprise, 'Of course not, but we really do need to know where you put it.'

'I walked to the shore, there is a little beach, over there.' She walked to the little white pained leaded window and pointed to the shore line.

'I put it in the water, but the tide was out, it was shallow, but the next tide would take it away.'

'Did you notice anything else whilst you were there?'

'No, nothing. What do you want to know that for?'

Milton thought about telling her about their enquiry but changed his mind, a look from MacLeod confirmed his decision.

'Nothing in particular, thank you for your help.'

They started to get up from the table when she stopped them, 'Where did you find the case?'

MacLeod replied, 'On the shore at Dunoon, it was washed up there.'

Mrs Lund thought for a second and said 'Hmm, near the body, I suppose.'

MacLeod stopped and Milton's head whipped round.

'Now don't look so shocked, the lady in the local shop told me, she was taking her husband to the ferry this morning and she was told by someone there that a body had been found. I may be getting on but I'm not senile you know.'

As they got to the door, Mrs Lund said, 'I heard a car about four o'clock this morning at the next cove, they tried to shut the doors quietly but I heard it. Didn't hear any voices or shouting, but I heard a car.'

MacLeod and Milton looked at each other and they sat down again. MacLeod said, 'Could you describe exactly what you heard?'

'Of course, but I'm not as spry as I used to be, I don't remember exactly what time it was, I think it was about four o'clock, I don't sleep that well since my husband died. I'll think about that, it was pitch black, I looked out of the window.'

She paused for breath but not long enough for either MacLeod or Milton to ask a question. 'I definitely didn't hear voices, it's a place where courting couples go, I don't disturb them, I remember my courting days, you know. Brings back memories.'

She paused long enough for Milton to say, 'Would you think about it and would you mind someone else coming round to take a statement from you?'

'Of course not, anytime, I'm usually in. Unless I'm dumping rubbish of course,' she giggled.

MacLeod and Milton managed to escape from the house but only after they had eaten their scones and drunk a second cup of tea. Outside the house they looked at each other and MacLeod said, 'I would have hated to have met her when she was younger, she wore me out today.'

Milton unkindly commented, 'Perhaps her husband died from worn out ears rather than a worn out heart.'

They went to the area where Mrs Lund had said she had thrown the suitcase, and found a small accessible cove, it was a very small inlet, only accessible on foot, with no sign of tyre tracks or unusual occurrence.

On to the next cove, some hundred yards towards Ardentinny and it appeared accessible to vehicles. They saw many car tyre tracks, and the latest appeared fresh. Access was difficult, but possible. The fresh tyre tracks seemed to belong to a heavy vehicle, possibly a Range Rover.

MacLeod did not get too excited about the type of vehicle. In these parts such large heavy vehicles are as common as saloons in a city. The weather made such modes of transport a necessity rather than a luxury.

At the shore Milton pointed to some marks on the rocks, they appeared to be splashes of blood. MacLeod pointed to a particularly blood-soaked tree. 'This will cut the overtime, I think we have found it.

Use my hand phone and ring the office, get the search team here, I want this area cordoned off for forensic examination. It could be a deer poacher, but I doubt it, they wouldn't bring a deer to this spot to butcher it, it's too close to the road.'

Milton walked back to the car, he had to plug in the booster aerial to get his message through, communications are difficult in the hills.

MacLeod stayed at the locus, he was too experienced an officer to move around too much and disturb what little evidence he could get. He wanted to be alone and catch his thoughts. The murderer must know the area fairly well to drive here in the dark.

It had to be a Range Rover type, it would be incongruous for a tramp to be seen in an expensive car, someone must have seen them. It's a pity Mrs Lund had not looked out of the window, she would have got the registration number, description of the driver, even his collar size before he left.

The most puzzling was why didn't the victim struggle or scream? He would know soon enough, the preliminary results of the tests could be through later in the day. He looked at his watch, It was later in the day than he expected. They would have to get back to the office to work out a strategy.

6

Doctor Muriel Lamont got off the plane at Glasgow Airport, she was exhausted, yet exhilarated at the day's meeting, she had met colleagues and friends from all over the world. She had caught up with the gossip, and had listened to the moans and groans of her recent colleagues.

The men in grey suits had taken over the NHS with a vengeance, she was pleased she had left the Charing Cross when she did. The move back to Cowal had been at the right time for all the family. John, her husband, had developed a thriving veterinary practice and her two sons had settled well into the local grammar school. Her inheritance had come at the right time.

As Muriel left the terminal building, she looked at her watch it was 9.30 p.m., an hour to get to the ferry. She wished the conference had been on a weekend when she could have caught a later plane, the last ferry would have been midnight.

It was only some nineteen miles but it was prudent to observe the speed limits in Greenock, the local police had a nasty habit of jumping out from behind buildings pointing a gun at errant drivers.

Muriel felt the faint pangs of hunger as she drove through Greenock, she did not enjoy airline food, she had a cup of coffee, it tasted stewed, but it was wet and warm. Lunch at the Ramada was a filling buffet, but she was talking and ate little.

She stopped at the Wee Chippy and purchased a fish supper, with a cold can of Irn Bru. As she paid she overheard two women in the queue talking.

'A murder, you say, in Dunoon, well it must be the first one in years.'

'No, not a murder, a body, my daughter lives in Dunoon and she rang me to tell me one had been found on the shore. Probably a drowning, fell overboard I shouldn't wonder.'

Muriel took her supper and left. She got into her car and regretted being at the conference, one day away and everything happens. She was the local pathologist and she knew that Alan Wood from the Inverclyde would have been called in. Muriel did not need the money but she needed the cadaver, it would have produced a sample for her research.

The ferry was nearly full on its last trip and within seconds of handing her ticket to the collector she was dozing, she had eaten her fish supper at the Quayside and the effects of a full stomach and a long day coupled with the gentle swell of the boat, she was gently rocked to sleep. There was a sudden thump and her car wobbled. She woke with a start, for a fraction of a second she was unaware of her surroundings and then realised they had arrived at Hunters Quay.

As she passed the Argyll Hotel towards her home at Innellan, she saw four tall men walking up the stairs into the hotel and recognised one as Detective Chief Inspector Cameron MacLeod. They had worked together on a particularly sad case some twelve months earlier and it came as a surprise, the body must have been the victim of murder. He did not turn out for anything less. She gave in to an urge to talk to him and parked the car outside the hotel. She would ring her husband from there, he would understand her curiosity.

MacLeod was accompanied by Hamilton, Reade and Milton. They had done as much as they could for one day, results from the fingerprint boys had recently been faxed to the station. The body was one Mary Bland; aged forty-nine years, of no fixed abode.

She had been arrested for petty crimes and had served thirty days only for shoplifting. Her antecedents were sketchy, she had provided a place of birth as Greenock on the 12th January, 1946, and was found dead within a matter of a few miles of her birthplace. MacLeod found this ironic.

MacLeod realised they would not be able to get home without driving all the way round the peninsular, it was cheaper to book into a hotel, rather than incur the mileage costs and Hamilton had his uses.

In the past they would have had to travel home, now it was a few pence cheaper to stay in a hotel they did so. He rang his wife from the station to tell her he would not be home tonight. She told him that everything was fine, he had two shirts and changes of underwear, if he was staying any longer he should tell her and she would come over to collect his washing and give him some clean clothes.

After he put the phone down he smiled, women, he thought, they care so much about clean underwear, he had to change and imagined he would be completely re dressed before he got to a hospital if he ever had an accident.

They booked in at the desk, they had been told that the kitchen had closed at 9.30 p.m. but fortunately had already eaten, the team had a Chinese take away at the office.

The Fiscal would be joining them at the Argyll, there was a small lounge at the back of the hotel, it was used for many a committee meeting, and the owners would make this available to them if asked.

No curious locals would be allowed to overhear their deliberations, the owners of the hotel were completely and utterly trustworthy, whatever they heard they kept to themselves.

As they were booking in Muriel Lamont approached them.

'What are you doing here, Doctor?' said MacLeod.

'News travels fast, I heard it as I was coming home.'

'Well, you may as well join us, the Fiscal will be here in a few minutes.'

He saw nothing wrong in inviting her to the informal conference, after all she should have been the pathologist on the scene and as they had the preliminary report it may be useful to have someone to decipher the medical terms, they knew most of the long medical words but sometimes they needed an interpreter.

MacLeod introduced her to the rest of the party and as they went to their rooms, she walked into the bar, ordered herself a tomato juice with a dash of Lee and Perrins and took it to the residents' lounge.

In the lounge there was an extension telephone, she picked it up and asked for her home telephone number. She was asked what room number to put it on. She thought for a second, 'Put it on Mr MacLeod's room, he won't mind.'

She spoke to John and explained what had happened, he sighed a little, 'Don't be out too late, and don't drink, you have surgery early tomorrow and so have I.'

He knew the hospitality of the police off duty, to his cost. He still remembered the hangover he had when the local sergeant had retired, a small 'do' had turned into a heavy session, with capital 'H' and 'S'.

'You know I don't drink when I'm driving, I won't be persuaded to drink, I'll be home in an hour.'

He laughed, he knew what an hour meant to his wife, she had no sense of time, 'See you when you get in, if I'm awake.'

Duncan Grey came into the lounge bearing a tray full of pints of beer and a whiskey for each pint. He saw Muriel relaxing in a comfortable chair, 'Didn't get you one, was told that you weren't drinking, you can buy your own, I don't get fruit juice at a bar, it would ruin my street cred.'

At that he sat down, 'Now why are you here, my lovely, I thought you were away in the big city.'

'Don't call me my lovely, I'm hardly a girl anymore. I was passing when I saw MacLeod walking into the hotel, I heard about the body in Greenock and I was curious. It's a pity I wasn't here, I like a good body.'

'Don't tell me porkies, you were miffed at missing a body, it's for your research, I will never know how a woman like you could poke around with blood and gore. The meaning of life is in people not what they are made of.'

'I was a consultant haematologist in London and old habits die hard but I'm not going to get into another argument with you. The last time was at the Burns Supper at the Masonic Lodge, it took all night. I can't explain it to myself never mind you. Change the subject, I was just curious and was passing.'

At that MacLeod, Milton and Reade came into the room, they glanced at the tray and took a pint of beer and a whiskey each. They sat down and after taking a thirsty gulp of beer, Milton said 'Chinese meals make you thirsty, I needed that.' MacLeod drank as if he had been in a desert and only stopped when his glass was less than a third full. He sighed and sat back into his chair. 'Expect two others here, they booked in earlier, Detective Inspector Janet MacBain and the other is Detective Sergeant Susan Lampart, they are titillating themselves.'

Muriel was anxious to talk about the body but MacLeod and Grey did not like repeating themselves and she patiently sipped her drink until the rest of the party arrived, listening to the chances of Scotland winning the Grand Slam this year.

By ten thirty everyone had arrived and the usual introductions were made. Detective Inspector Janet MacBain was a woman in her mid to late thirties, she was tall and plump, and wore dark clothing to disguise her love of good food.

She was unmarried and many had made the mistake of looking at the body rather then the person behind the face. She had a pretty face, she appeared to be a solid housewifely person, an earth mother type and in another life would have had a brood of children clinging to her skirts.

She disguised a razor-sharp brain behind her outward pleasantness and very little escaped her notice. She had an affair with a married police officer early in her career, carefully concealed from her colleagues, which had ended in disaster.

Always one to learn from her mistakes she refused advances from everyone else, thus she became known as frigid or a lesbian. Neither was true. She was a private person and kept her home life just that — private.

In contrast Detective Sergeant Susan Lampart was a divorced woman, she had two children being looked after by their father and new wife.

She had access at weekends when she was not working and the situation suited her. She married a colleague whom she met at the Police Training School at Tullialan and once her probationary period had been completed she left soon after to have two children in quick succession.

On her return to the police force mainly due to financial reasons more than anything else, she saw little of her husband as they were on opposite shifts and days off. They grew further and further apart and soon divorce loomed on the horizon.

Susan became friendly with one of her colleagues on shift, an older woman, and realised she was a lesbian and felt freer than any time in her life. Fortunately her husband fell in love with a nurse at the Southern General and he asked for a divorce. She did not tell him of her life change, he would not have understood.

She liked his second wife and it was an amicable enough divorce, she allowed the children to go to their father without too much fuss, They would be better looked after at the new home. She kept her sexuality secret, the police service does not tolerate deviancy but some of her closest friends knew and turned a blind eye.

Hamilton started the meeting. 'All here then, Mr MacLeod would you brief the Fiscal to get us up to date.'

'Mary Bland, a woman of forty-nine was washed up on the shore at the old changing rooms in Dunoon. She was of no fixed abode, she had been stabbed repeatedly, but there was no sign of defensive cuts therefore she was either drugged or rendered unconscious by other means before she was stabbed.'

There was a knock on the door, the waitress brought sandwiches complements of the hotel, Mrs White the owner was, as ever, a proper host.

MacLeod went on after she had left, 'No blows were inflicted on the head. She had no money in her pockets only a piece of paper with the numbers five-six-seven-two. They have been checked, all local numbers are six-figure numbers and the four figure end numbers in Glasgow are now being run through the computer.'

He paused and looked at Doctor Lamont, 'Are you okay, Doc, you look tired.'

'I've been up since five thirty this

morning, I think I need a drink to get me going, tomato juice isn't doing me any good.'

Grey said 'Right its on me, I'll get the waitress.'

He rang the bell and when the young waitress arrived he said, 'Same again, except for the tomato juice, she'll have a . . . '

'Gin and tonic.'

MacLeod went on, 'We found the locus in a small bay at Ardentinny, quite secluded. She had been stabbed with a long thin blade.'

He shuffled papers and said, reading from them, 'Entry between the sixth and seventh rib on the left side with an upward thrust into the heart was the cause of death. She had been in the water no longer than twelve hours.'

He paused and Doctor Lamont said, 'Quite accurate, a lucky stab I should think, any more information?'

'No, there were other wounds eight or nine in number, a passionate killing. How on earth could this woman cause such a passion in anyone is beyond me.'

Detective Inspector Janet MacBain was carefully examining the photograph in the file, 'Had this woman had children?'

MacLeod said 'Hang on a minute.' He turned the page and said, 'There's something here.'

He handed the pathologist's report to Doctor Lamont.

'Hmm, yes she had more than one child.'

MacBain then looked up, 'It's the Duchess, she was a pain in the lower regions when I was a peewee, she was always coming in telling us her children had been kidnapped. I thought I knew her face.'

Milton took the picture from her and studied it, 'Of course, a right nutter, although she was passable when she was young. She was a prostitute on my beat. I thought I knew her.'

Hamilton interrupted, 'You all know her, why don't I?'

MacLeod was sorely tempted to say that he had as much chance of meeting a street woman as he had flying to the moon when he spent all his time in the office or on courses from being a young copper, but he resisted. He merely said, 'Perhaps she didn't move in your circles, sir.'

Reade in his quiet laconic way said, 'We have the means, she was stabbed, we have the opportunity, anyone could have taken her from the streets of Glasgow, we have not many suspects. We just don't have the motive.'

Milton, who had a habit of stating the obvious, said, 'Once we find the motive, we will narrow down the field. The Duchess was well-spoken, she must have come from a good family at one time, we will have to start real police work and dig it out. Someone must know her background.'

He turned to Detective Inspector MacBain, 'You and Detective Sergeant Lampart, go back to Glasgow in the morning, and find the tramps and street girls who might have known her. I always know who to give the exciting jobs, dress for the part, will you. Get the first ferry, the tramps are up early.'

Detective Inspector Janet MacBain and

Detective Sergeant Susan Lampart looked at each other. They knew that MacLeod was a one off, but they were now convinced that they were working for a madman. Up late at night and out early in the morning, he certainly expected his pound of flesh. They finished their drinks and left without a word.

'What are your plans now Cameron?'

'Someone must know of this woman, she must have come to their notice sometime. Detective Inspector Reade will liaise with you as soon as we get some information. Perhaps Constable Morris will come up with something from his little computer, you never know.'

Muriel Lamont had continued reading the pathologist's report and told the assembled company, 'Oh! There is one more thing I forgot to tell you. If she hadn't been killed she would have died soon anyway, her liver was about to give up, she didn't have long to live. This murderer couldn't have known that, all he had to do was wait. It's one of those things, life's a bitch. Anyway I'm bushed, I will get off home now, if there is anything you need me for I will be more than willing to help, but I think you won't need me any more.'

She left, as she was walking out of the reception she stopped and said to the receptionist, 'I feel a little guilty about putting my phone call on Mr MacLeod's bill, I'll pay for it.'

The receptionist smiled and said, 'That's all right Doctor, I told him when he came down and he said it was okay so long as you were not ringing Australia.'

She heard gales of laughter coming from the lounge, another session was about to begin, the men were more comfortable on their own, business was concluded and they were about to relax with a vengeance.

7

Janet and Susan were at the ferry at 6.15 a.m. They had travelled to Dunoon the previous day in Susan's car, Janet had left hers at home.

Whenever they had been working together they worked as a good team. They had been assigned to some weird cases in the past, some were routine murders but the cases they both hated were anything to do with abuse of children, it made them both feel nauseated.

Janet moaned at Susan, 'I know now why I hated early shift, this isn't a time, it's a disease.'

'I don't know, it was nice to finish at two, and any overtime was paid for, not one in three hours and even then we have to beg.'

'Would you like to go back to Uniform?'

'Not yet, I love what I am doing and it

fits in with getting the children when I'm not on call. I liked uniform work, but I think I like CID better, despite pigs like MacLeod.'

Janet burst out laughing, 'He wouldn't like to hear you calling him that, I've worked for him before, he knows what he is doing. The trouble is, he doesn't tell you what he is thinking and you have to work it out. He's a pussy cat really under all that growling. Don't try to pull a fast one, he has a memory like an elephant.'

'And looks like one too,' murmured Susan. 'I hate fattism, we all can't be beanpoles like you.' Susan looked at Janet and her eyes widened, 'I didn't mean it like that, oh dear, foot in mouth syndrome again.'

As they waited for the ferry they were approached by a bored looking constable with a clip board, 'Excuse me, were you on this ferry yesterday?' MacLeod's instruction to have every car and person interviewed was being carried out to the letter, unfortunately for this officer, he had his cap on the back of his head and was chewing gum.

Janet became suddenly official. She showed him her warrant card and said, 'No, we were not, and I think if you were properly dressed and ate your breakfast before coming on duty you may get a better response from the public.'

He looked at the card and put his cap on properly, he took the piece of chewing gum from his mouth and threw it into the water.

'Sorry, Ma'am, I didn't know you.' He flushed a bright pink.

Susan thought Janet was being a little hard on him, from the 'bum fluff' on his face he must be a probationer nearing the completion of his probationary period.

When they got on the ferry she commented, 'A little tough, weren't you?'

'Maybe, but he has to learn he could be talking to anyone.'

'Today he was,' grinned Susan.

They went to their homes and dressed down for the occasion. They both wore jeans and sweaters to go out on the streets of Glasgow, both had worked in uniform in this area and headed for the 'Tramps Hall' as it was known locally, a charity run by the Church of Scotland.

Most of the local down-and-outs went there for breakfast, a cup of strong sweet tea with a lump of bread and soup of the day, it was made with whatever could be obtained cheaply from the local market early in the morning. It cost the clientele nothing, all that was asked of them was that they turn up sober and cause no trouble.

Janet approached the staff behind the counter, she asked if the supervisor was in. The supervisor of the hall was a formidable lady of indeterminate years, she had been a person of wealth and position and was always known as Sister Jenny, her surname was never used.

She had funded 'Tramps Hall' and maintained it from her inheritance, when she had seen the unfortunate tramps living and dying on the streets of Glasgow.

Most of her fortune had gone into such work, and as she had never married, she would have become a nun, but she felt that the restrictions of Holy Orders was not for her. She preferred to work alone with a little help from the Church.

Once she passed over to a better place, she would leave the rest of her money to the Tramps Hall to keep her work going, but how long the money was to last was of great concern to the Church Elders. Sister Jenny had no such concerns — God would provide.

Susan went off to find anyone who knew the 'Duchess' preferably one who knew of her background.

The main hall was quiet and each table was occupied by one tramp, such persons are not gregarious and prefer their own company. Life on the streets had taught them to be suspicious of everyone, even their best friends could steal from them if a pair of boots or a warm blanket is the means of survival on a cold winter's night.

Janet was taken into a small but neat office at the rear of the counter, she was greeted by Sister Jenny, who rose from her seat.

'Janet, it's a long time since I've had the pleasure of your company. Now, what can I do for you?'

Janet and Sister Jenny had met before Janet had even considered a career in the police force, she had been a child of these same streets, her parents, now dead, were staunch members of the Church.

They had moved to the area before its slow decline into poverty, they refused to move even when it became quite obvious that it was an unsuitable place to bring up a child.

Janet enjoyed the diversity of the area and the friends she made helped her considerably when she joined the force.

She was known and friends were willing to give her information, other officers were impersonal faces in a blue uniform. Janet was a friend, even though she had gone over to the other side.

Janet kept her faith with her friends, she never arrested one of them. However she did pass on the information if necessary: she would not turn a blind eye to criminal behaviour, it was just she had some scruples when it came to arresting her informants and school friends.

Janet sat down with Sister Jenny, she felt as if she were back in the old Bible

Class days, she sat up straight and felt slightly uncomfortable. She showed the picture of the 'Duchess' to Sister Jenny, who took it from her.

'She was found in Dunoon, she was stabbed. I'm sorry it had to be a photograph after death. Do you know anything about her?'

'I liked her, a wayward child but she didn't deserve to die like that.'

Sister Jenny went silent, Janet knew enough not to push her and the silence lengthened. Suddenly Sister Jenny said, 'Excuse an old woman's eccentricity, I was thinking about her. I'll tell you all I know.'

Sister Jenny sat back comfortably in her chair with her eyes closed and her fingers entwined in front of her waist.

Janet had a small tape recorder in her handbag, which has become an essential tool of CID work, she asked and was given permission to use it and she set it before Sister Jenny on the table.

Sister Jenny told Janet that she remembered a young prostitute named Mary Bland, she was, unfortunately addicted to alcohol. She lived with a boy called Jimmy Bland and took his name, she had two children and they were running the streets at the age of two and three. They were ill-fed and waited for their mother outside the local pub.

The Green Man it was called in those days, it has changed hands many times and the new name escaped her. The children were taken away by the social workers and it took Mary a couple of days to notice.

Mary came to her to ask if she could try to get her children back, really it was the first time she had spoken more than a few words.

Sister Jenny had learned early in her career not to try to change any of her 'parish', God came into their lives without her help, or didn't whichever the case may be. She set an example and hoped that was enough.

Sister Jenny was taken by the refined accent of this young woman and asked her where she came from 'Nowhere, no one wants me so nowhere,' was all she said then.

When Mary had to attend Court at a custody hearing Sister Jenny had stood with her, she held her in her arms as Mary cried after the judgement. It was decided that the children would be better off in the care of the social workers.

After her sobbing had subsided, Mary merely shrugged her shoulders and left to the nearest pub to have a drink as if nothing had happened.

Mary took up with another pimp called Walter Rose, and bore another child, but this one was taken into care at birth. Mary took to the drink with a vengeance and Walter eventually got fed up with her. He threw her on the streets with only the clothes she was wearing.

Sister Jenny saw Mary more often when she began to live on the streets and only once did Mary ever open up and actually have a conversation.

It was then she told Sister Jenny that she had been at boarding school in England and had an unfortunate affair when she was young, she had a baby and the child was adopted. Her future husband was killed in an aeroplane crash.

Mary rambled on about the wedding she should have had and the life she missed. She said he was an American serviceman, an officer, she called his name Dave or David, Sister Jenny was not quite sure.

It was the only time Mary ever showed any outward emotion and tears had welled in her eyes, but she was careful not to allow them to take her over.

Up to a couple of weeks ago that would have been all the story, but last week Mary came into the hall and told everyone that she was going to get her money, what was due to her and she would never see this place again. Mary left and Sister Jenny never saw her again.

Janet had listened intently to the story Sister Jenny had told and did not interrupt once. Sister Jenny was never one to embellish a tale neither would she forget anything interesting. Janet asked, 'How do you remember all this?'

'My dear, it isn't often you get a woman like her on the streets of Glasgow, I have often thought about her. She was introverted as most of my clients are, until something happens to trigger them off and they talk, really talk and I listen. I felt Mary had never spoken to anyone for years.'

'Did you find out where she came from?'

'Unfortunately not, Mary would not answer any questions about her family, I asked her but she did not answer, I felt that I was listening to her thoughts, I suppose I happened to be there rather than a two-sided conversation.'

Janet was about to turn off the tape recorder when Sister Jenny said, 'It's strange you know, I've had a private detective round asking for Mary last month. I told him the same thing I told you. A coincidence I believe, he didn't tell me why but it could have been something to do with her family. Perhaps she had come into money as she said. I thought she was safe, but alas, not to be.'

She went to the top drawer of her desk and gave Janet a business card: 'JOSEPH ARMSTRONG, PRIVATE DETECTIVE, 115 JAMAICA STREET, GREENOCK.,'

Janet took the card with thanks, 'Can I

come back to see you if I need to?'

'Of course, my dear, if I remember anything else I'll get in contact through the local boys.'

Janet walked back to the main hall and saw Susan who looked up with a desperate pleading in her eyes. 'Get me out of this' was easily seen from the look.

Susan was being regaled by an old and very smelly dosser about nothing at all, he was still drunk from the night before, he was rambling and attempting to touch Susan to her obvious revulsion.

Janet hesitated and thought about leaving her there, she had a warped sense of humour, but decided that Susan seemed to have had enough. She nodded to her and Susan managed to get free and they left the hall.

Susan was scratching her arm and shoulder, 'I think I've caught something.'

'You may have, always keep three feet away from them, I'm told fleas can't jump that far. Did you get anything, apart from nits that is.'

Susan ignored the last remark. 'They all know her but no one has seen her for a couple of days. That last dosser, he's called the Galloping Major. Don't any of these tramps have names? Well, he said he saw her at the Central Railway Station, he thought she got into a car, but he didn't know when it was, nor did he know what kind of car, and he didn't see the driver. He was pissed at the time.'

'Language! Susan, This is a Christian hall.'

'Sorry, but I think he was having me on. Mary was supposed to have a bottle of Scotch in her pocket, he followed her because he saw it and was hoping to get some. Fat chance from what I've found out about her. He saw a car draw up, Mary was called over by name, and she got in. I ask you, his imagination got carried away with him, it must be the DTs.'

'It's all right, we can always contact him again to be properly interviewed when he sobers up, he's a regular.'

Susan scratched herself, 'I'm not talking to him again 'til he has a bath. You know I saw the nits swinging from strand to strand of his hair.' She shuddered, 'I could hardly hear what he said, I was looking at his hair.'

Susan went on, 'He wouldn't come to the station to give a statement, he won't go near the police voluntarily, I don't suppose the locals will go near him voluntarily either. I'm glad you came when you did, he was trying to get more money from me, I thought a fiver was good enough for what he told me. If he's right, which I very much doubt, he's given us a start. We'd better get the British Transport Police and ask if they know anything. What about you?'

Janet briefly told Susan what she had found out whilst they drove to Glasgow Central. The British Transport Police knew their patch inside out, maybe someone had seen something, but she wouldn't hold her breath. They would ring the office from the BTP Station. They had a start but it was tenuous.

8

'Detective Inspector MacBain has rung in. Sister Jenny has come up with a lot of useful information and a private detective called Joe Armstrong has been making enquiries about her too.' Reade gave his report to MacLeod and Hamilton.

'Not old Joe, I thought he was dead,' interrupted MacLeod.

Hamilton said, 'You know this man?'

'Of course, he retired a few years ago, he was built into the foundations of Pitt Street, Milton and I will follow this one up, Joe can be a little stubborn you know.'

'Sergeant Milton, get your bag, we are off to Greenock, another ferry ride.'

He turned to Hamilton and Reade, 'I'll ring you to keep you updated, excuse me sir, we will be off.'

MacLeod and Milton left the office before Hamilton had time to say anything. MacLeod hated flying a desk, he was a hands on detective, paper work was necessary but not his favourite occupation.

They left with almost indecent haste. Sergeant Gillespie saw them leave and turned to his two constables who were standing in the main reception, 'Okay, pay up, I told you he wouldn't last more than two hours in the office, never bet with an expert.' He took his winnings with relish.

* * *

Jamaica Street is a narrow cobbled street which used to be part of the bustle of the town. Since the new shopping centre opened at the other end of town it has become a backwater, like a beached whale flapping uselessly to try to float on light waves lapping on the shore.

Its shops are run down, like the rest of the town. The closure of the shipyards hit Greenock, at one time nearly ninety percent of the men were unemployed. Recently there seems to be an unaccustomed buoyancy, work was gradually coming back, in the new computer industry and the inhabitants were feeling a little more optimistic.

MacLeod and Milton climbed a long, dusty stair to offices above the cheap clothing shop in Jamaica Street. The door to the office was out of a story book, the words etched on clouded glass proclaimed, 'JOSEPH ARMSTRONG, PRIVATE INVESTIGATOR'.

They entered and found Joseph sitting at his desk piled high with files. He was smoking a cigar and had a hot steaming mug of coffee in his hand. 'Been reading too many detective novels, Joe, where's the beautiful blonde secretary?'

'Gave her the day off Cameron, anyway an answerphone is more accurate. How are you, long time no see, what do you want?'

Armstrong got up from his desk and extended his hand, they shook hands vigorously, they were old friends.

Armstrong looked over MacLeod's shoulder and exclaimed, 'John, you old scroat, bag man again I see.'

He gave Milton a friendly pat on the shoulder, and he visibly staggered.

Armstrong was a big man from the Hebrides, as many of the old-time police officers were. He was over six feet tall, he was well built and showed his boxing experience on his face. To say that he was ugly was an understatement. He did not have much trouble on his beat, no one was prepared to take him on, drunk or sober.

'Would you like a coffee, I've had to give up the drink. My doctor has given instructions and he has a nasty habit of calling in when I don't expect him, so the drink has gone.'

MacLeod was relieved to hear this; Joe had a deserved reputation for his over-enthusiastic hospitality, no matter what reason or what time of day it was. They accepted and soon they were sitting comfortably in front of a warm gas fire, holding steaming mugs of coffee.

'Now, what can I do for you, it must be important for you to come and see me, Cameron. It's not a social visit is it?'

MacLeod told Armstrong about the body found at Dunoon, Joe nodded, 'I heard, but then everyone must know by now.'

MacLeod said, 'She was Mary Bland.'

He waited and was satisfied to see Armstrong sit bolt upright in his chair, 'Mary Bland! You found her for me then.'

'Come on Joe, what do you know, and why were you looking for her?'

'I can't tell you, client confidentiality you know.'

MacLeod's eyes narrowed, 'Friend or no friend, I have to know, there's a murderer out there, do you want to be locked up until you do tell me?'

Armstrong gave a loud belly laugh, 'You know I will tell you, but I have to put up a little bit of a struggle, I have to keep up appearances. All right, I'll get the file and you can take out of it what you want, I have a photocopier in the corner under the stairs, I hope it isn't being temperamental. Let me have the originals back, I need them.'

Armstrong went to his desk, lifted three files and gave MacLeod the file marked 'Mary Abercrombie'.

MacLeod jumped out of his seat,

'That's it, that's where I know her, it wasn't in Glasgow as a prostitute, it was at Innellan. Mary Bland is Mary Abercrombie!'

The other two men looked askance at MacLeod, they had not ever seen him like this. MacLeod was overjoyed, it was as if he had been worrying at a problem and now it was solved.

'Calm down, man,' said Armstrong, 'We aren't getting any younger you know, your heart can't stand such an exhibition, neither can mine. What are you talking about?'

'Sorry about that, I went to school at Dunoon Grammar when I was a lad and worked part time as a groom for the Abercrombies. Mary lost her temper with me one day, she hit me with a whip. Her father was furious and made her apologise to me. If you could have seen the look on her face, the apology nearly choked her, she could have killed me. A stuck-up bitch that one, but she was beautiful and she knew it.'

'You a groom, Clydesdales I suppose?' Armstrong retorted.

MacLeod ignored him, or did not hear him, whichever, and continued, 'I left as soon as I could. I didn't see her again, but she left to go back to school and wasn't seen again. I didn't expect her to turn up dead, a down and out, she had money and everything she wanted.'

Milton having seen the photograph of Mary was a little sceptical about MacLeod being right on this occasion. However, he was prepared to give him the benefit of the doubt and did not interrupt. 'She did me a favour though, if she hadn't belted me with the whip I may have been working there yet, I joined the army the following year and the rest is history.'

Armstrong was a little contrite, he knew that the first twenty-four hours in a murder case was vital and he was apologetic, 'I should have contacted you about her. I'm sorry if it delays your investigation but it took me a long time to get what I did.'

MacLeod was not one to bear grudges and said, 'Come on, Joe, give me the facts from the file, you know I hate paperwork.'

'Well, my client is an American, Clara Croft as she was, Clara Chambers as she is now. She had a brother who was an American serviceman killed in an air crash when he was on his way back from here. He was in some kind of disgrace because he had an affair with a young woman, he wanted to marry her and the family didn't approve. They didn't know who she was and paid me handsomely to find out, I told them it was almost impossible but they gave me the money anyway.'

'I never knew you to give up cash, but you seem to have done well on this case.' MacLeod was delighted to have this information so early in the enquiry.

Joe rose to the bait and almost shouted, 'I'm not tight fisted, you've still got the first penny your grandmother gave you, Cameron. Where was I? Oh, yes. This brother didn't tell anyone who she was and his father regretted not finding out about this young lady, he wanted to make it up to her, he told the sister on his death bed and made her promise to find her. If the girl was happily married she was to leave it be, he didn't want her to cause any problems. If she was unmarried or in dire straits she was to make her life better by making sure she had enough to comfortably live on.'

'If they had found her it would have made her last days happier instead of the way she went,' Milton observed.

'Clara came over with her husband last year. She didn't have any names or anything else except his age and date of death. To cut a long story short, through some friends in the US Naval Investigating Service, I found his best friend who had given the keys of his flat to Dave, he told him he had a girl and needed space. He didn't say who she was but I saw some of the older residents and they told me the only strange disappearance during that time was Mary Abercrombie. There was some comment when she didn't turn up for her father's funeral.'

'Typical,' commented MacLeod, 'you can't do anything there without someone knowing.'

'I traced a taxi driver who eventually told me that he had taken her to the unmarried mothers hostel in Glasgow, he promised not to tell but as old man Abercrombie had died he thought it would be all right to tell now. After she left the Southern General she disappeared.'

Milton got up from the chair and made another cup of coffee for each of the men, he was thinking of the change in lifestyle from rich to poor, it was surely easier the other way round. Perhaps MacLeod was right about her after all.

'I went back to my old haunts and found a woman who remembered a well spoken tart called Mary Bland. I didn't know this Mary at all and Sister Jenny told me the rest. I didn't try to see her because my client said she and her husband were coming over for a holiday and were doing Europe. They were due to come and see me last week and we would decide what to do then. They didn't come, I'm waiting for a call. That's about it my friend, the rest you can find in the file, there isn't much more.'

MacLeod was full of admiration for Armstrong, he was what was known as a ferret, he had learned a lot from him as a young copper, and was learning more. Perhaps retirement could be just as interesting as working in the police force.

'What do you do apart from this sort of thing, Joe?'

'One of these cases come up once in a blue moon, mostly I interview witnesses for the defence or prosecution, or I serve warrants when the Sheriff's officer is too busy, I tick over and mostly am bored to death, but it's a living.'

Milton photocopied the whole of the file and gave it back to Armstrong.

On the way back to the car, MacLeod decided that he had to eat, he thought about going to a restaurant but decided to get a takeaway black pudding supper and go home. His wife would be at work and he did not know much about being in the kitchen, it was a family joke that he needed a diagram to find his way there, but he could manage a cup of tea.

At the kitchen table Milton said to MacLeod through a mouthful of black spicy pudding, 'This case was getting to be easier, someone else had done all the leg work, at least it saves us a lot of time and effort. Detective Superintendent Hamilton will appreciate that, the overheads would be less.'

MacLeod was glancing through the file, he saw that Joe Armstrong was as meticulous as ever. Everything was noted down and he said, 'Having seen this file a prolonged enquiry of this size could only be done by a Private Detective such as Joe. With the state of the police service at the moment I doubt whether the public purse could afford it. We could have done it but it would have been a struggle, we would have been told to wrap it up long before we got anywhere.'

MacLeod began, for the first time, to mentally compile a list of suspects. He never jumped to conclusions, some of his colleagues tended to find a suspect and then tried to make the evidence point to that person, most of the time they were correct, however when they got it wrong, disaster could occur and the whole of the police service paid the price.

9

When MacLeod and Milton returned to the office he handed Hamilton the file. It was very thorough, Joe Armstrong had not only carefully and meticulously recorded every detail of Mary's life, he had found out the dates of birth of all her children. Armstrong obviously still had contacts in the Social Services Department and he had sight of her file. He had not taken copies of the pages of the file but had enough time to make detailed notes.

MacLeod thought that Joe's network of 'friends' was as vast as his own, but MacLeod could not get on with Social Workers no matter how hard he tried. He knew they did a good job, but some looked on the police as 'the enemy' and treated them accordingly. MacLeod had been unfortunate in meeting this type on a regular basis. His view was strictly biased.

Hamilton was taken aback at the date of birth of the male child, no one except his closest family and friends knew that he was adopted. He shared the same birth date as the son of Mary Abercrombie. He heard little of what MacLeod told him, the date made a sound in his head and that was all he could concentrate on.

MacLeod said 'Are you feeling all right, sir, you seem to be a little out of sorts?'

The question penetrated Hamilton's thoughts. 'Oh. Fine. Yes, I'm all right.'

MacLeod was not content with this, Detective Superintendent looked a delicate shade of grey and MacLeod was genuinely concerned. 'I'll get you a cup of tea,' and he left the office.

Hamilton thought about his happy childhood with his parents in Bridge of Weir. He knew he had been adopted from the time he could walk, his mother had told him.

The way it was explained to him was simple, other parents had to take what they were given, but he was special, he had been chosen by them. Hamilton had neither the urge nor the inclination to trace his birth mother, as far as he was concerned the couple that had brought him up were his parents, it was as simple as that.

When MacLeod left the office to go to the incident room, he allowed himself to breathe properly again. This ravaged soul could have nothing to do with him, he had thought of his birth mother on occasions but never could he imagine her as an alcoholic tramp who made her living as a prostitute. No this was too much, he had to sort this out, he trusted MacLeod enough to confide in him. He could never be a chief constable with this on his record, as usual his thoughts were purely selfish.

When MacLeod returned with the tea, he cleared his throat, 'Please shut the door, I have a little problem, I hope you can be very discrete, no one else must know.'

MacLeod was a little confused, Hamilton confiding in him. This was a first, 'Now what' he thought, but said 'Go ahead, I'm always discrete, if there is something to keep quiet then I will.'

'I don't know how to put this, but I was adopted and you know it is a strange coincidence, but the date of birth of this tramp's baby is the same as mine.'

He hurried on, 'I know I can't be her son, after all, look at me, but it's a coincidence, isn't it?'

MacLeod was completely taken aback, he did not know what to say, in fact he was, for probably the first time in his police career — speechless.

MacLeod finally said, 'We'll be investigating what happened to all her children, I don't believe in coincidence and it would be too farfetched if you were her son, many children were born on that date all over Scotland, I wouldn't worry if I were you. If it did turn out you were her child,' he changed his tone to a more formal manner, 'Could you please tell me where you were on the night of the fifteenth?'

Hamilton stared at him in horror and then realised MacLeod was attempting to break his mood, it succeeded, 'Out, and take your questions with you!'

MacLeod said gently 'I hope she was

not your mother, I know what this could do to you.'

As MacLeod left the office he met with Doctor Muriel Lamont in the doorway.

'I was in the station taking blood samples from a drunk driver, Sergeant Gillespie told me that you had identified the body, he said it was Mary Abercrombie.'

'Yes, that's right.'

Muriel Lamont sagged a little, 'She was my cousin, she ran off years ago and we thought she was dead.'

MacLeod helped her to a chair, 'I'm afraid not, could you recognise her to make a more formal identification?'

'We were the poor relations, my father and Mary's mother were brother and sister, we lived in the same place but we moved in different circles. Father and Aunt Jane did not get on well so I only saw her at Christmas and birthdays for a duty visit. I don't remember much about her at all.'

Muriel was handed a cup of tea by Constable Milton who had seen her buckle at the knees. Hot and sweet, the great British pick-me-up.

Her hand shook as she took the tea, and was steadied by MacLeod.

'Do you feel up to answering some questions now, or should we leave it until later?'

'I feel all right but I don't know what I can tell you, I haven't seen Mary for, let me see, for over thirty years.'

'Mary said that her father had left her some money and she was going to be rich, or that is what she told the people at the Hall, do you know anything about that?'

MacLeod was sparse with the details.

'I was told that her father refused to declare her dead after such a long time. I was invited to the house some years after Mary vanished and treated as the daughter they never had, it was my good fortune in a way that Mary went off. I didn't know she had become pregnant nor that she had any children, she simply was not discussed. It was through Aunt Jane that I was put through university and I was made heir to the fortune only when Aunt Jane had Mary declared dead.' Her voice trailed off.

MacLeod persisted, 'Did you know what Mary meant when she said she was getting her father's money?'

'I really don't know. Perhaps she was in the last stages of dementia, they go like that you know. I didn't expect the money, nor did I want it. If I'd known of Mary's circumstances I would have gladly given everything to her.'

'Where were you on the night of the fifteenth, Doctor?' MacLeod was gentle but firm.

'Now look here, you don't think I had anything to do with her death do you?'

'Of course not Doctor,' said Hamilton, 'but we must ask the question of everyone who had a motive, and from what you say, you certainly have one, after all if Mary had turned up out of the blue, it really would put you in an awkward position.'

'Oh. I see, I was at home, I had to get an early night, I caught the early ferry to go to a conference in London, you all saw me in the evening in the Argyll, or was the session too much for you and your memories are a little shaky?'

MacLeod winced, he remembered it too well, in fact he was still feeling the effects somewhat. Muriel seemed to shake herself and stood up.

'You know where I live and you can contact me anytime. I must get on, I have a surgery in half an hour, must look my best for my patients.'

As she was about to leave MacLeod said, 'If you inherited all that money, why are you still working?'

This was a question which brought a little light relief to the proceedings.

'It's the Scottish work ethic thing, I suppose. Anyway I don't have all that much, my private laboratory at home takes a lot to run, I'm a researcher at heart but this way I can do what I want without all the politics of grovelling for finance.'

Hamilton and MacLeod nodded their heads, they knew exactly what she meant.

'John, my husband, is a vet and he shares the facilities, for his business. We are comfortable and would never have been able to do it without the money but

I'm a healer not a killer.'

MacLeod said, 'Would you recognise her if you saw her?'

'I'm afraid not, I was only a child when I saw her last, but if she is positively identified please tell me and I will make arrangements for her funeral. I think it is only fair I should do that. After all she was family no matter what she had become, or how she ended her life.'

Doctor Lamont put her shoulders back and said as she walked to the door, 'If there is anything else I can do, Chief Inspector, don't hesitate to ask.'

10

The murder squad assembled in the incident room. The atmosphere was subdued. They sat at desks with papers in front of them and, although they could be congratulated for the results up to now, they felt they were no further forward in finding out the perpetrator.

Each piece of information was merely a background of the woman but no obvious suspects had come into the frame.

Constable Morris was the first to give his report, 'I've checked everything I can think of, but this number is completely useless. I can't think of anywhere else to check.'

There was a wry smile on the face of MacLeod, he and his older colleagues were none too conversant with computers and he felt that nothing could replace the human mind, although the computer boffins thought they could.

He was right of course, computers are

tools, to take the mindnumbing drudgery out of any work, police work was no exception.

'I've checked every telephone number in the country and even the International codes.'

Morris on his own with the aid of a computer had checked every telephone number in the country, a job that would have taken months manually.

'There was a Glasgow number but it was an artists shop in the St Encoch Centre, no one there had seen Mary nor had heard of her. The alibis of the staff had checked out. No one had even heard of her.'

Morris had, in desperation, even checked with Newcastle, HQ of the Department of Social Security, hopeful this could be an emergency number, it proved fruitless.

'It could be a lottery number except there were only four figures,' said MacPherson.

'If you win, tell me, Constable, I don't want a postcard from the Bahamas. We will have to get a replacement.'

MacLeod was semi-serious and the mood of depression lifted in the room.

'I think you have done the best that you can, Morris, I think carrying on would be fruitless, there's plenty to do.'

'Oh! No, sir. I would like to get to the bottom of this. It must mean something.'

'Fine. But put this one on the back burner. Other jobs have priority.'

MacLeod saw that Morris was crestfallen. 'Some you win, some you lose, son. You'll learn.' he thought. MacLeod turned to Detective Constable MacPherson. 'Your report now.'

'I have interviewed the boys, they could not add anything to their original statements, except that the body was not there the previous evening. I took a policewoman as requested, they seemed more frightened of her than me.'

He smiled broadly. WPC O'Neill was a formidable lady and gave an air of authority that over rode her appearance. It was pleasant for someone else to be the 'heavy' for a change.

'The shore is their playground. They had been in the changing rooms area

116

until approximately twenty-two hundred hours the previous evening and would have noticed if she had been there then.'

'Did you get round to see Mrs Lund?' Milton was checking off his list of things to do.

'Yes, we went straight there after we had seen the boys. WPC O'Neill and I finally managed to fix the time at around 2 a.m. instead of 4 a.m., she remembered looking at her clock. That would fit in with the tide turning, but otherwise Mrs Lund could not add anything to her statement. But her home baking was lovely and her home made strawberry jam is better than my grandmother makes.' MacPherson had a dreamy look in his eyes as he remembered the feast.

MacLeod frowned at MacPherson, he appreciated levity, but not at a briefing. He would have to have a word with the young man afterwards.

Detective Inspector Reade updated the squad with the results of the forensic tests. It was confirmed that this was the place of death.

'The tyre marks are from a Volvo

Estate, not a Range Rover. The tyres were relatively new and no unusual cuts or markings are discernible. There are approximately three hundred such vehicles registered in the Cowal Peninsular.' He sighed, such vehicles were as common as Ford Escorts in the City.

'We are getting a full printout from the Police National Computer through Police Headquarters at Pitt Street. Once the list comes in we will have to start prioritising for further enquiries.'

Detective Inspector MacBain said, 'I'm sorry but there is nothing else from what we already know. The BTP had a very quiet night on the day that Mary was murdered and we can't confirm what the Galloping Major told us. They did say they threw him off the station, but no one saw Mary. She was well-known but wasn't seen. I have had a message from the front desk. Sister Jenny wants to see us apparently she has remembered something else, but won't tell the local police so with your permission Mr Hamilton, we will go and see her now.'

Hamilton thought about it for a

second, 'No. Go tomorrow, you have done your eight hours now.'

'I don't get paid for overtime,' replied MacBain.

Lampart interrupted, 'I'll go for love not money, I won't claim anything.'

'The DI and I can go home afterwards and it won't cost another night in a hotel.'

Hamilton considered this, 'All right, I'll see how much we have left and tell you what you can claim.'

MacBain and Lampart left the office. Janet turned to Susan, 'I like the hotel, it's great food and well looked after, but I'd much rather be in my own bed. Thanks Susan, I owe you one.'

After they left, MacLeod turned to Detective Inspector Reade, 'Give us a suspect, anyone will do, I feel we are walking through porridge.'

'Well, I was going to tell you that Doctor Lamont was the next of kin, but it seems that she has upstaged me. I have made enquiries at the hospitals in Scotland and fifteen boys were born on that day and of these twelve were adopted. That's without any private adoptions which may have been made, I'm afraid we can't trace those. The adoption agencies are reluctant to give any details, but at least we can find out where Mary's children were adopted.' Reade frowned.

'What's the problem Mr Reade?' MacLeod was always formal in the presence of junior officers.

'The Social Services have the records but they will not tell us. No doubt they will tell the Fiscal. I will ask him for a warrant to get the information.'

MacLeod nodded, pleased that they seemed to be getting somewhere, even though he felt they were clutching at straws.

Reade went on, 'I've checked that Mary was officially declared dead in 1990, and I've also had the will of Mrs Abercrombie faxed from the Public Record Office in Edinburgh. It seems that Muriel Lamont was the sole heir, to the tune of two million pounds in cash and estate.'

He paused and waited for the infor-mation to sink in to his audience. He was suitably satisfied at their reaction.

Hamilton sat up straight in his chair, MacLeod's mouth fell open. He murmured 'Comfortable, that's what she said, comfortable. I'd hate to know what she thinks is rich.'

MacPherson nearly dropped his coffee and Morris's glasses slipped down his nose making him look more owlish than ever, Reade continued, 'I haven't read the will through as yet, but I gather Mary's father was an astute businessman, although no one would know by the way they lived. Rich enough, yes, but not that kind of money.'

MacLeod said 'I expect anyone would feel tempted for that kind of money. Get their alibis checked out thoroughly, Constable MacPherson.'

He looked at Reade, 'Anyone else?'

'I contacted Heathrow and Mr and Mrs Chambers came into the country on the twelfth of January, they have a visitors permit for six months, I checked the hire firms and they hired a Volvo Estate from Avis at Heathrow for five months. They got a green card insurance to travel on the continent and paid in advance. It seems that Mr Chambers is well off, he is a lawyer from Baltimore, USA. He has taken early retirement because of ill health and they are touring Europe.'

Hamilton couldn't help himself and said, 'How on earth did you find this out?'

'I asked the girl I spoke to, she had never taken a hire for this amount of money before, he gave an American Express card and she had to get authorisation before he took the car. She seemed a pleasant chatty girl, she nearly had my life story before she finished. Anyway, she remembered both of them very well.'

MacLeod wondered if Hamilton had ever made an enquiry, he instructed Reade, 'Find out if they have booked accommodation in Scotland through the tourist agencies or Trust House Forte, they could have an itinerary and we could find out where they are now. Otherwise it will have to be an all forces alert. I take it you got the registration number of the car?'

Reade nodded and said, 'That's about

it. I've covered everything.'

'Is there anything else?' asked Hamilton. When there was silence from the room he continued, 'I think we should not forget that she was a tramp, she had the whole world as her enemy, I want the Galloping Major interviewed again. It may be that they came over to this part of the world on foot, the tyre marks could be perfectly innocent.'

MacLeod was furious, Hamilton had to learn that nothing is 'perfectly innocent' in an enquiry until it was proved to be. He should never, never express an opinion like that in a briefing, the team could downgrade an important point on the opinion of a supervisor. Consciously or unconsciously they followed the lead of the man in charge of the enquiry, no matter how inexperienced he may be.

MacLeod tried to minimise the harm and support this man, he turned to Detective Inspector Reade, 'Get the ferries checked, two tramps would be remembered. They may even come by road, but I doubt it. He may have killed her, he had a motive if she had a bottle of whiskey. I won't exclude anyone at this stage. When the girls ring in, tell them to get hold of that tramp and really interview him this time. I'm sure they will enjoy that. Keep me informed if anything else comes up.'

Detective Sergeant Milton said to MacLeod, 'Do you want the new 'action sheet' made up now?'

'Yes, we will go through it and see what else is needed.'

MacLeod looked at his watch. He had time to get the ferry and go home, he said to Hamilton, 'I want to review the information, I could go home but I feel it would be more productive to stay another night in the Argyll.'

'I think so too, we'll both stay, if there is a room that is. Detective Inspector Reade, do you want to stay?'

'If it's all right by you I will go home, my wife has some sort of Perfume Party and I said I would look after the children, she was going to get the neighbours to babysit, but I'd rather go home.'

MacLeod understood Reade's dilemma and ever the one to think of his staff's welfare he turned to the rest of the team.

'After we have finished the 'action sheet' the rest of you get home and have a good night's sleep. It's going to be a long boring day tomorrow. All leg work and we know how frustrating that can be. Thank you for what you have done up to now. I think we are getting somewhere.' He sounded more optimistic than he felt, but it was unwise to pass on his morose thoughts.

'I'll contact the hotel, it's getting towards their busy period, I expect they will be pleased there are only two of us.'

A lot of the leg work had been done by Joe Armstrong, 'Good old Joe' MacLeod thought. All they had to do now was to wait for something to turn up and the jigsaw would soon be completed.

11

Janet and Susan arrived at Tramps Hall about 7 p.m. Much to their annoyance it was closed. Janet decided that they should return early in the morning to see Sister Jenny, whatever she had remembered could wait. They both needed a good night's sleep after such an early start. They hammered on the door but there was no answer.

'That's unusual,' Susan remarked, 'Sister Jenny doesn't leave here until eight o'clock at the earliest.'

'Well, she has left early today and I think we should go home too.'

'I don't know, Janet, the message seemed urgent.'

'Do you know where Sister Jenny lives? No? And neither do I. She has never given anyone her address. We'll see her in the morning.'

Janet reasoned that they would be more alert in the morning, a decision which would have disastrous consequences.

Hamilton and MacLeod had a good meal at the Argyll, steak pie and the trimmings, a speciality of the house of which they were justly proud.

After coffee in the lounge overlooking the Clyde river, the lights of Gourock and the steady blink-blink of the Cloch Lighthouse steadied Hamilton's nerves.

He was pleased to hear that so many other baby boys had been born on the same day as himself. He knew he was not the child of this tramp, despite the fact he could be a rich man if he were, or could she be his mother? He shuddered at the thought.

He turned to MacLeod, 'If I were her son, could I inherit?'

'A moot point, I don't think so. I don't think you could inherit because you were adopted, from the little I remember of adoption, you sever all ties with your previous family.'

MacLeod was not too sure about this, it was something he would have to check, if the child could inherit he would have to eliminate any other children who turned up from the enquiry.

'The sin of avarice rearing it's ugly head, is it?'

'Of course not. I just thought about it.'

MacLeod thought that perhaps any one of her children could think the same thing. They would have to find them all.

'I wonder, I'll have to ask the Fiscal when I see him, if she were declared dead already, how can you murder an already dead person? It must have happened before, or has it? It's going to be interesting though — we may make headlines yet.'

'So long as it isn't that woman who interviews us.'

* * *

He still couldn't bring himself to mention Helen MacDonald's name, she really had an effect on him.

About 10 p.m. there was a noise from the reception area, they heard women's voices, the waitress came over to them and said quietly, 'There's been a girls night out, one of the nurses at the hospital is celebrating her birthday, your peace and quiet is now shattered, if you don't want to get involved I think you should nip out the back way.'

They recognised Helen MacDonald's voice, 'speak of the devil' said MacLeod.

They both decided that a gaggle of women was too much for them. They crept, like guilty schoolboys, out of the side door and into their rooms.

Hamilton needed some time on his own to think about the events of the day, particularly how it could affect him personally.

MacLeod went to bed, he had an ugly thought rearing in his head. He had to be alone to review the day's events. He held his tongue when Hamilton asked about the money.

He wondered where Hamilton was the night before the body was found. Perhaps he had been the son of Mary. But no, that was too much of a coincidence and MacLeod did not believe in coincidence.

After all he had, for the very first time, taken personal charge of this enquiry. Could it really be that this man could commit murder to protect his career? MacLeod thought not, but there had been murders in the past for less.

They had adjoining rooms and said goodnight at the door. They each had a magnificent view over the Clyde, but neither man saw it. They were too preoccupied with their own thoughts.

Hamilton finally got to sleep about 1 a.m. The beds were comfortable and big, he was lulled into a fitful slumber, he saw Mary's face in his dreams, she faded in and out of his consciousness.

MacLeod was going through the will of Mrs Abercrombie. She had made a codicil indeed making Muriel Lamont the sole heir, but that was in 1991.

However, when he read the main body of the will, it stated that should Mary's child be found, whether it had been adopted or not, he or she was to inherit and Muriel was to gain £200,000 from the Estate.

MacLeod knew that Mary could never inherit, despite her announcement to the rest of the homeless.

So Muriel was inheriting a large sum of

money even if a bastard child was traced. It seemed that there had been the minimum of enquiries as prescribed by law to trace both Mary and her child.

It took a coincidence by the appearance of Clara Chambers, born Croft, to give the case a boost.

MacLeod was opening the file given to him by Joe Armstrong when he heard a noise from the room next door, there was a thump as if someone had fallen out of bed.

He became alarmed and rushed to Hamilton's door and knocked, 'Are you all right sir?'

He heard signs of a struggle and he knew something was wrong. He forced the door open and saw Hamilton lying on the floor.

He was holding his neck and blood was spraying out of a wound, over the bed and furniture. He looked at Hamilton, his eyes were wide open, pleading to MacLeod. He was desperately clutching at a wound in his neck, the blood was forcing through his fingers. He was going into shock.

MacLeod saw a dark figure at the window climbing on to the fire escape. He thought about following but he knew that Hamilton was dying and needed his immediate attention.

He grabbed a towel and applied pressure on the wound, Hamilton lapsed into unconsciousness.

MacLeod grabbed the telephone, pulled it towards himself and called for an ambulance and police.

It seemed like hours before anyone came. He was praying that Hamilton would not die, he was shocked at the attack, nothing like this happens in Dunoon.

MacLeod could only think that this was a sneak thief who had been disturbed, but the figure in the window was slim and dressed in black.

Hamilton must have been attacked when he was asleep. This couldn't possibly be anything to do with the murder of Mary, or could it? This deed was utterly motiveless, or so it seemed.

The light was suddenly switched on and he saw Mrs White, the owner's wife, an efficient and capable woman. She saw that the need was indeed urgent. She was a nurse before she married and became a hotelier.

Mrs White took hold of the situation, and carefully took MacLeod's hand from Hamilton's neck.

'I'll see to him, you did well to stop the bleeding but you will kill him if you keep that pressure up on his neck, leave it with me.'

MacLeod gratefully handed his charge over, he looked round the room. There was blood everywhere, the floor, walls and even ceiling. It seemed that the whole room was bathed in Hamilton's life-blood.

Mary was murdered in a cove, trees and bushes were covered with blood. The similarity did not escape MacLeod's attention. His imagination took him to the cove, he saw the slash that severed her carotid artery and the shadowy killer watching her life's blood spurt before other stab wounds were inflicted on the dying woman, including the death blow through her heart.

This killer liked his work, they were looking for a psycho and no mistake.

There was no reason for the attack on Hamilton, perhaps the killer got the wrong room, he MacLeod could have been the target. He shuddered at the thought.

The local police and ambulance arrived at the same time. There is an ambulance stationed at Dunoon Hospital for emergencies, however this was the first time they had anything like this.

MacLeod told the first constable he saw to secure the room and stand by the door until forensic could be called, and told the second one to go with Detective Superintendent Hamilton and stay with him, not to let him out of his sight.

He thanked Mrs White and apologised for the need to keep the room isolated.

'Could you hurry, I don't want my other guests disturbed.'

'I'm sorry but we will have to interview your guests, you never know someone may have seen something.'

Mrs White sighed, 'This isn't going to help my business, but if you must, you must. I'm up now so I'll get you a list as soon as possible.'

'Could you get a list of everyone who was in the hotel tonight, I know there was a hen party in, we heard them.'

'I'm sure Iris will remember, she closed the bar about midnight. They must have all left by then.'

MacLeod regretted the decision to let most of his team go home. He would not be able to sleep now and decided to change, he was covered in blood, he had to change into the casual clothes he had brought with him. He would have to go home and get clean work clothes in the morning. He drove to the police station where he saw the station Sergeant, Sergeant Mulligan.

MacLeod was told that the road to Glasgow had been blocked as soon as he called for help, no one had driven up the road. This was the only road from the Cowal Peninsular, a great help when the ferries were not running. Dunoon was now isolated; if the perpetrator were to escape this was the only road.

'What about the town?'

'Nothing is moving, if anything does we will soon get him. He must have gone to ground, he must be hiding, but it escapes me. I have had all the taxi drivers seen at the rank, they will bring anyone covered in blood, or even the slightest bit suspicious, to the station.'

The taxi rank was in the main street and most of them were on duty until the early hours of the morning, if anyone saw anything they would without hesitation tell the police.

It wasn't worth the aggravation if they did not.

'I will go to the hospital and see how the Detective Superintendent is getting on, I can't do anything here.'

'I've contacted Force Information Room, the top brass are being told, if they ring, what shall I tell them?'

'Everything we know, it isn't much, we'll get all the staff and overtime we need now.'

He felt the irony of the situation, money would be poured into this now, Hamilton was worth the money, poor Mary was not.

MacLeod went to the Accident and Emergency department, he saw Hamilton lying on a trolley, he had been seen by the duty doctor and an emergency operation had been carried out whilst he was on the trolley, he was too ill to be moved.

MacLeod saw Doctor Lamont and was a little startled.

She said, 'Don't be surprised, I have to stay overnight in the hospital when I am on stand by, we don't have the money for permanent doctors, the day shift is done by doctors from the Inverclyde. I'm quite capable, you know.'

Hamilton was very pale and she was carefully, almost tenderly wiping his face, he had a saline drip in his right arm. She looked up at MacLeod.

'You saved his life, I had to put sutures in the neck wound, I'm afraid he has lost a lot of blood and I want him over to the Inverclyde as soon as possible. We can't cross match his blood here, and he needs it fast, he's lost a great deal you know. The Western Ferry is on stand by and we are taking him there now.'

She put her hand on MacLeod's arm,

'Go get some sleep. Go on or I will have two patients on my hands.' She shooed him towards the main doors.

'Will he be okay?'

'Oh, yes. Once he has been topped up there should be no problem, but he is going to be off duty for some time until we can assess his case. He is in good hands, now go back to the hotel and get some sleep or I will have two patients on my hands.'

MacLeod glanced in the mirror and saw that he was definitely a peculiar shade of grey. He grunted and returned to the hotel, everything that could have been done was being done for now. He would be in the way, he had to trust everyone else, but he felt so useless.

He put the files away, if he started reading them he would never get any rest. He went to bed and got a fitful few hours.

He couldn't help thinking about Hamilton and the grisly scene. Perhaps he himself was the real target, and every noise woke him. At 4 a.m. he rose and decided to get the rest of the team out of bed, he was up, they should be up.

They would get as good a start as they could before the nine o'clock shudders, 'You should have done this, you should have done that', a trait of all bosses from all walks of life, not just the police service.

12

Janet was awakened by the telephone at the side of her bed. She looked at the clock, it was 4.15 a.m. She sat up in shock.

Hamilton had been attacked and she was needed in Dunoon as soon as possible. She asked if Detective Sergeant Lampart had been called, she was told not yet, she told the caller from the Force Information Room that she would ring her and get her out.

Janet rang Susan and told her to pick her up as soon as possible, they would drive round to Dunoon, it would be quicker than travelling to Gourock and waiting for the first ferry.

Susan was at her flat by 4.45 a.m. and they were quiet, both were thinking about the Superintendent.

Susan drove over the Erskine Bridge and was driving along Loch Lomondside past Duck Bay Marina before she broke the brooding silence.

'Who would want to try to kill the Super, he couldn't have made that many enemies,' she paused and said 'yet.'

'Somehow, I think it is something to do with the case, I think this female had a past which we haven't really touched on.'

'Hamilton is about the same age as her son, he couldn't be him, could he?'

The atmosphere was broken, Janet had a vision of Hamilton calling Mary 'Mummy' and started to giggle. She had an infectious giggle and Susan tried to suppress her mirth but soon was laughing out loud.

If MacLeod had seen these women laughing whilst driving through Tarbet and Arrochar he would not have been amused. As they drove through the wild mountains from Arrochar on the Inverary Road, their mood changed. The laughter was a form of hysteria, no police officer likes to hear of another being hurt, especially the way Hamilton was.

Mindless violence is part and parcel of their jobs, but this was a personal attack, it always made everyone else nervous and a little jumpy.

The view over the Rest and Be Thankful is one that can turn the head of the most travel-weary. The view down Glen Kinglas towards Inverary is one of the most beautiful in the world, however today both their thoughts were elsewhere as they turned left to Dunoon.

Susan and Janet lapsed into their own thoughts for the last twenty-eight miles of their journey and arrived at the police office at 6 a.m. Susan was not one to stick to speed limits when it was safe not to, if a 'black rat', or to give their proper name, the traffic police, had tried to stop her they would have had a good chase on their hands.

Susan had been a 'black rat' at one time in her career and had been taught to be a fast, safe and good driver. Janet rarely felt unsafe in her capable hands, and had settled down in her seat. She didn't even notice the winding road past Lock Eck where many an unwary or tired traveller had crashed the lochside barrier and ended up in the Loch's dark waters.

On arrival at the office they found Detective Chief Inspector MacLeod sitting at his desk. He was not looking too well; his face was ashen and he was wearing a pair of grey flannels and a casual shirt, with a tie of course.

His appearance gave both women a shock, they had never seen him in anything other than immaculate, tie, crisp shirt and smart suit, usually blue pin striped.

He looked at them and saw their expressions 'I have to go home on the first ferry to get clean clothes, my others are bagged as productions, there may be some evidence from the perpetrator.'

He thought for a few seconds, neither women thought it prudent to interrupt, 'Now I need you Janet, to take over until Peter arrives, he will do everything necessary in the office, he is a brilliant office manager, you two are better detectives on the street.'

MacLeod paused as if to collect his thoughts, the attack on Hamilton had severely shaken him, more than he cared to admit.

'I have had time to write down my statement, everything is here. Go to the Argyll and interview the residents as they get up. Mrs White will give you all the help you may need. After that sort out the list of non-residents she will give you and get them interviewed. You had better see Helen MacDonald, don't tell her anything more than necessary, she's a very good reporter drunk or sober.'

MacLeod picked up his case and was walking towards the door when he turned and said, 'Ask Mrs White for our bills, I'll settle them when I get back.'

Neither Janet nor Susan had spoken a word whilst MacLeod had been talking, they realised he was shaken and they could get all the information they needed at this office. After they left they looked at each other, Janet said, 'Did he call me by my real name?'

'Yes, and he gave us a compliment I think.'

'He must be ill, I hope he manages to get a rest, I don't think I can stand a compliment as well as him remembering my proper name. Well, let's get on with it.'

They sat down at the two senior officers' desks and began to read the reports of the night before. They had just started when Detective Constable Milton arrived. He wore glasses and always looked like a frightened hamster to Janet. 'I drove round, but not as fast as you I see.'

Janet was a great believer in finding out as much as possible before setting out on an enquiry, every little helps was her maxim, whereas Susan believed in the intuitive method of work. She needed very little information to make a leap of faith into the unknown and come up with the right answer. Sometimes she was wrong but not often.

Suddenly Susan looked up, 'Oh, shit, Sister Jenny!'

'She will have to wait, we have more important things to do.'

'I know, I know, but we should see her, can I go? I have a feeling in my bones she should be seen soon, don't ask me how but I just know.'

'Okay, I know you, but I can't let you go and see her, we would be off the force and in Civvy Street next week if we don't do this job.'

Janet looked at her watch, 'Sister Jenny should be in Tramps Hall by now making the soup, I'll get a local to call round and apologise for us and tell her we will be there as soon as possible. If a WPC goes perhaps she will talk to her, she prefers talking to women.'

Janet made a call to the local police station, she spoke to WPC Connie Mason and explained the position. Connie had been in the force for some twenty-five years and was well known to Sister Jenny, she had joined the force when the Equal Opportunities Act had not been implemented. She regretted the demise of the Policewomen's Department, all the unsung work done by the peewees had fallen by the wayside to a large extent.

The job was turning full circle and a department staffed by both women and men had to be resurrected to do the work of the old Policewomen's Department. She had been asked to join this new Department but had declined, she had begun to enjoy being the 'mother' of her shift and felt going back was not for her.

Connie had never had any aspirations for promotion and felt a sense of pride when one of her 'chicks' got on. Janet was one of her babies of whom she was justly proud. She would pop round now to see Sister Jenny, after all she would get a good cup of tea when she was there. She called to her newest charge, Constable Frank Nisbett, three weeks from the Initial Course and very, very keen. She would have to slow him down sometime and thought it was about time he was introduced to a local celebrity.

They went to Tramps Hall, it was only a couple of blocks away from the station, and Connie decided to walk. Frank was a little miffed, he liked to sit in the police car, the shell around him felt comfortable and he felt safe. He had not yet become so used to his uniform that he felt safe walking the streets. He walked stiffly beside Connie, and hoped that no one would ask him a question or that anything would happen.

It was to take some time before he realised that no one asked a policeman anything on the beat except the time and the way to the nearest public convenience, and the chances of him falling over an incident was remote, he would usually be sent by radio and he had time to think before he got there. This beat was real life, not the made-up events played out at the Training School.

They arrived at the Hall by 6.30 a.m., and Connie stopped in her tracks, 'The doors are closed, no lights on and I can't smell cooking. Something's wrong. You stay here, I'll go round the back.'

She went round to the side door, this had been a church hall at one time and the pathway had been used by many feet. It had worn in some places but Connie was used to such rough ground, many a pair of tights had been ruined by a stumble. She was careful where she put her feet, it was almost by instinct she carefully put her foot down on the path before she let her weight fall. She got to the back door and saw a gleam of light from the kitchen, she stood on tiptoe and looked in.

The sight that greeted her was to stay

with her for the rest of her life. Sister Jenny was sitting in her chair at her desk, she was lolling to one side like a rag doll, her eyes were staring and her mouth was open, a small dribble of blood came from her lips, she had a gaping wound on her neck caked in blood. The light from the desk lamp glowed eerily on her pale blue skin.

Connie looked round the small part of the room, she was horrified to see dried blood on the walls, it was as if someone had sprayed the blood from a spray can, a ghoulish graffiti artist like no other.

Connie was too well trained to enter the scene of death. She knew Sister Jenny was dead and that there was nothing that could be done for her. She called on her radio for assistance, this incident was for the CID. She heard her probationer fall as he came quickly round to her. She sighed, he was like a puppy, he hadn't even got his legs yet, she hoped that he had not disturbed any evidence. He arrived looking somewhat flustered.

'Stay here, don't let anyone in and

don't look inside. I want you alert when the CID arrive.'

Connie went round to the front entrance to direct the inevitable cavalcade of CID, forensic, senior officers, etc. All thoughts of breakfast disappeared fast. She wished she had eaten before she left the station, or, on second thoughts, perhaps it was a good idea she had only a cup of tea; she was a friend of Sister Jenny and was feeling sad at her loss.

A lump came to her throat, then her mood changed, how could anyone harm this lady? Anger took over, she could think better angry. Sadness only clouded her mind, she would have time later to grieve.

Connie suddenly heard a noise of retching. 'I told you not to look, perhaps you will listen to me now.'

Constable Frank Nisbett had seen his first murder victim and was throwing up in the bushes, he would have some explaining to do to the forensic boys when they came to the scene. Connie smiled, I probably shouldn't have got a boy to do a man's job.

13

About 8 a.m. the same day, Detective Sergeant Janet MacBain was sitting in the Argyll Suite of the Argyll Hotel. It had been set aside by Mrs White for their purposes, she did not have many residents in the hotel and allowed them to have breakfast in the Clyde Suite before ushering them into Janet and Susan.

She had a telephone call from the police station and called Janet to the telephone in the reception hall.

It was Detective Inspector Peter Reade, 'Janet, I'm sorry, Sister Jenny had been found murdered. She has been stabbed, her carotid artery had been cut, but the PM would give the actual cause of death later. It appears to the attending police surgeon that she had been dead for approximately twelve hours.'

Janet felt tears prickle in the back of her eyes and a lump in her throat. She felt weak at knees and leant against the wall.

The shock was overwhelming for a fleeting moment, it was closely followed by a surge of anger, 'Why would anyone want to murder a woman like that? She had no enemies. Perhaps it is connected with her wanting to see me.'

'Hurry interviewing the guests and get back to the incident room asap. It could be a coincidence that Sister Jenny had asked to see you.' Peter Reade was as pragmatic as ever.

Janet went back to the Argyll Suite where Susan was finishing an interview with an elderly couple on holiday from Sheffield. As they left the husband said, 'We won't be moving out, Mrs White is worried we all will. Well, we came for a holiday and nothing like this has happened to us, we may even stay on for a few more days. We can dine out on this for years.' They left arm in arm.

Janet told Susan about Sister Jenny. Susan stood up and began pacing the room, 'I knew I should have gone to see her today. I knew it. I knew it.' Susan was distraught.

'It would have been no good, she has

been dead for at least twelve hours, we must have called on her shortly after she died. We are going to have to think about it; did we see anything, did we miss anything and why on earth did we only go to the front and not the back?' Janet was clearly upset. Susan stopped pacing and said, 'We weren't to know.' She paused and stared at Janet.

'How about this as a what if! What if the murderer was still in the hall?'

'Detective Sergeant Lampart,' Janet became suddenly formal with her colleague. She thought that Susan was about to fall apart.

'Get a grip, we have a job to do and we cannot allow our feelings to interfere. I'll give you a few minutes to sort yourself out. We have other things to do. And don't even think we could have saved her we weren't to know this could happen.'

'I know that but someone is going to say it. I feel so helpless and angry with myself.'

'We'll just have to get hold of ourselves, we have to get back to the station as soon as possible, how many more residents have we to see?'

'Only one other couple, Americans, they arrived about 9 p.m. last night, they are going to stay for a couple of days.' She looked down and said, 'Oh my God! I didn't notice, it's Mr and Mrs Chambers, the ones we have been looking for all over Europe, they have turned up here and I really am being dense.' She smacked her forehead.

At that a middle-aged, but very smart lady came into the room, she was accompanied by a tall distinguished man of ruddy complexion, slim with a shock of white hair. It seemed as if he were prematurely white, his skin clearly matched a younger man's hair. He was casually dressed in light trousers, unsuitable for the raw winds that sweep up the Clyde, and a lightweight polo-necked jumper. She was dressed in a dark knitted dress, it had obviously been purchased recently at one of the ubiquitous Woollen Mills which have sprouted all over the country to cater for the tourist trade.

Mrs Clara Chambers spoke in a well-educated American accent, and said,

'Can we help you officers?'

Janet replied, 'There was an incident here last night, can you remember anything out of the ordinary?'

'I'm afraid not, we booked in and went to bed early, we had a terrible drive from Oban, there was an accident and we were held up for some time, my husband needs to rest after being stressed out and we simply went to bed. I believe I was asleep by ten thirty.'

Mr Chambers then said, 'That's right, I was asleep before Clara. I need my sleep, I'm an eight hour man.'

Janet considered telling the couple that the police were aware that they had hired Joe Armstrong, and the result of his enquiries, but thought better of it. She had a gut feeling that MacLeod would want to see them and that it would be prudent to leave him room for manoeuvre.

'Will you be here for a while, someone else may want to talk to you later.'

'Well, we have to go to Greenock sometime, but I want to look round here today, I suppose tomorrow will do, another day won't make any difference.'

Mr Chambers said to his wife, 'After all I want to show you round.'

He turned to Janet and Susan, 'I was here in the Navy you know, I didn't last long, not cut out for that kind of life. Tomorrow will do, yes, we will be free. I am under instructions from my doctor to rest in the afternoons, so I expect we will be here around threeish.'

Janet and Susan hurriedly packed up their briefcases and left. As they were leaving Janet remembered to ask Mrs White for MacLeod's bill. Mrs White gave a peremptory wave of the hand and said, 'Later, I know where you are, you won't run away. I haven't got the time now. It will be waiting for him whenever he wants to call round. I've cancelled Mr Hamilton's bill.'

Janet said, 'You don't have to do that.'

'Oh yes, I do,' retorted Mrs White, 'He was hurt in my hotel, I hope you get whoever did this before me.'

She left the threat hanging in the air. Janet believed that she really could harm anyone who brought shame or harm to *her* guests.

They got back to the incident room to find the place in turmoil. Woman Constable O'Neill brushed past them as they reached the door. She said over her shoulder, 'That was nice. But I'll tell you when.'

Detective Sergeant Milton was convulsed with laughter, his head in his hands on the desk. Detective Constable MacPherson was holding his face and a reddening mark was spreading over his right cheek. Detective Constable Morris was sitting at his computer desperately trying to give the impression that he was concentrating on his work.

Detective Inspector Reade appeared from the inner office doorway and said, 'What's going on? What's all this about? Come on, John, get a grip and tell me.'

As WPC O'Neill walked past Janet and Susan, she winked and continued down the corridor. She appeared to be laughing.

Detective Sergeant Milton finally managed to speak. 'MacPherson caught a right hander, that WPC thought he had 'goosed' her and she flattened him.'

'Is that right!' Detective Inspector Janet MacBain was horrified. Sexual harassment in the police service was regarded as a sacking offence.

'No. I never touched her. She scares me, I don't know what happened.' MacPherson was shocked and horrified at the suggestion 'She just hit me.'

'It's my fault,' a little voice interrupted.

Everyone looked at Morris, incredulous that he should actually do something out of character.

'I turned round and she was behind me, I didn't see her and I wanted to attract the Sergeant's attention but I waved my arm and touched her. It was an accident and I didn't have the courage to own up. I'm sorry,' he turned to MacPherson, 'I should have told her, but she scares me more than anything.'

MacPherson looked at his partner with sympathy. Reade said to Morris with a little compassion, 'Don't worry, if she had hit you she may have killed you. MacPherson is big and strong enough to take it. Now what's all the fuss about?'

'I thought I could see a pattern and I got into the Social Services computer.'

'I don't want to know,' said Detective Inspector Reade as he turned on his heel and returned to his office. Bravery and going against procedure was not his idea of good police work. What he didn't know wouldn't hurt him.

'Go on,' Janet was interested.

'Sorry, but when all the fuss started I inadvertently hit the wrong button and I've got to start again.'

This was one of the occasions that Detective Inspector Janet MacBain wanted to strangle someone, and Morris was that person. She took a deep breath and said, 'Try again, son. You may have something, and I'll be waiting to hear from you.'

Shouting at Morris was not the way to get him motivated, he simply would not respond and may even freeze with fear. Patience was needed in these circumstances.

14

MacLeod let himself into his house as quietly as he could; he didn't want to wake everyone up. He wanted a short time on his own before the hectic routine of breakfast. He went into the kitchen and saw his wife and children eating breakfast.

'Early breakfast then.'

'Daddy!' shouted Jacqueline and she jumped up and knocked the breakfast table.

Morag said, 'Jacqueline for goodness sake!' and grabbed the milk as it was about to spill.

Jacqueline ignored her and ran to her father to give him a hug, closely followed by Nicola. 'Whoa, I've only been away for a couple of days. It isn't pocket money time yet, is it?'

Morag looked at him with some relief. 'We heard on the news that a policeman had been hurt in the Argyll Hotel and was in the Inverclyde. I told the girls it couldn't be you because we would know before the radio.'

He made a mental note to change the girl's alarm clock from a radio alarm to an ordinary bell type. He could imagine what had happened after they had heard the bulletin, he was glad he was out.

'Bad news always travels faster than good, you know I can look after myself.'

But he gave the girls an extra bear hug, he was somehow pleased at the welcome home. It was normally an 'Oh. You are back.' and he was lucky to get a kiss on the cheek.

Morag said, 'Leave your father alone, he is tired and it's nearly time for school, so off upstairs and get your schoolbooks.'

As they untangled themselves from their father they kissed him. Nicola whispered, 'Don't let anything happen to you, Dad.' and followed her sister up the stairs.

After they left Morag hugged him and said, 'Why didn't you ring and tell me you were all right?'

'I honestly didn't think of it, I knew

you would have known I wasn't hurt. Next time . . . '

She interrupted, 'There won't *be* a next time.'

She extracted herself from his arms, 'Sit down, you look awful, have you had any breakfast?'

He shook his head, 'I don't feel like any, a cup of coffee will do.'

She looked at him and said, 'Cameron MacLeod, you will have breakfast and then lie down for a couple of hours, they can do without you for that long.'

Morag was in no mood to be argued with. He drank the tea he was given, Morag did not believe that coffee was good for anyone first thing in the morning. He was going to tell her he had been up since 4 a.m., but thought better of it.

Morag was concerned about the cholesterol level in his blood and usually gave him a low-fat breakfast: cereal, low-fat milk and toast.

Today she excelled herself, the Sunday treat had been brought forward: bacon, eggs, soda scone, black pudding and square sausage. He wasn't hungry until he looked at the plate and as he was about to start his substantial breakfast, the telephone rang.

He sighed and was about to get up from his chair when his wife said, 'I'll get it, eat your breakfast while its hot.'

She answered the phone and he heard a one-sided conversation.

'Yes, he is here,' pause, 'He is very tired, can he come out later?' another pause, 'Yes, I understand, but please, can he eat his breakfast first?'

She smiled and turned to her husband, 'It's Assistant Chief Constable Mackenzie for you, he says you can finish your breakfast after he has spoken to you.'

MacLeod took the phone from her, 'What can I do for you, sir?'

'A formidable lady, your wife, she should meet mine, like peas in a pod, or perhaps they shouldn't, we don't want them comparing notes. To business, a Sister Jenny has been found murdered this morning, the preliminary report shows that she was killed in the same way as your body, and the attack on Hamilton.

'I want your report as soon as possible, but I do want you to go to the locus in Tramps Hall, you may see something others may miss. After all you have already seen one body and one attempt so it may help if you see the other.

'I've given instructions for Janet MacBain to pick you up as soon as she can and take you there. I don't want you driving so take what rest you can, she'll be with you in about an hour.'

All MacLeod could think to say was, 'Whatever you say, sir.'

He was too tired to argue, he would feel better after his breakfast and a short nap. He could work for days without a proper sleep, taking an occasional nap, it was fortunate that he could in this job.

MacLeod was asleep when Janet and Susan arrived. Morag gave them a cup of tea and gently woke her husband. He got up, shaved, dressed and came downstairs, he looked as if he had just slept for eight hours, he was fresh and ready for work.

Morag said, 'I've packed another case for you.'

'I won't be needing it. I'm coming home tonight.'

'Put it in the car, you never know.'

Janet and Susan were startled at the appearance of MacLeod, they had seen him exhausted only a few hours ago, now he looked as if he could run a marathon.

On the way to the car Janet muttered to Susan, 'I wish I looked like that after a night's sleep. It's going to be a long day.'

On the drive to Glasgow, MacLeod asked, 'Why are both of you here?'

Susan replied, 'It's my car and I'm the only one insured for it.'

'Or could it be that you are like all females, don't want to miss anything? Now catch me up with your enquiries so far.'

They did so, and he was disturbed to hear that the wandering Americans had arrived in the hotel, it was a bonus he didn't expect.

He was pleased with Janet's decision not to tell them of the result of Joe Armstrong's enquiries. He would tell them himself as soon as they got back to the hotel.

It was busy on the M8, they slowed to a crawl near the airport and it was start-stop all the way to the Kingston Bridge. Susan knew this area well and decided to take a different route at junction 21, she was a little impatient during a rush hour and would rather go a longer way round rather than wait in a queue, at least she would be moving.

'Have we any further news about the car that picked up Mary at Glasgow Central?'

MacLeod's memory was prompted as Susan drove under the railway bridge.

'No, we thought the Galloping Major was imagining things, we have had an all points out for him, but he hasn't turned up yet,' said Janet.

'You know these tramps, they sometimes drop out of sight for weeks and then turn up again like a bad penny,' remarked Susan.

'I know, but after Sister Jenny's murder, I'm getting a little worried. Perhaps the murderer didn't expect Mary to turn up on the beach and is now covering his or her tracks.'

'Her?' said Janet, 'It would have to be a strong woman to attack the Super.'

'I know, but the Superintendent's attack could have been unrelated by another person, using the same MO. That clown MacDonald had the details printed in the local paper. I saw it this morning. I will strangle the person myself who gave out the details,' said MacLeod.

Janet said, 'Detective Superintendent Hamilton was the only one who has given an interview with her. You don't suppose he told her do you?'

MacLeod considered this for a moment and said, 'I will have to ask him when he comes round, won't I.'

Susan said, 'Why do you think a woman could be the murderer?'

'I don't really, but if I say 'him' all the time, it cuts out half the population, I don't want to appear sexist.' MacLeod was almost diffident.

Janet looked at Susan and grinned. Even he was coming round to equality, but he wouldn't admit it.

At Tramps Hall, WPC Connie Mason was still at the entrance, on guard. She had been given a spell to have a cup of tea and something to eat, but was back on duty when they arrived.

Janet went up to her, 'I'm sorry Connie, I didn't know.'

'I bet you didn't. My new proby has been well and truly blooded, you owe me one.'

They went through the police tapes and donned the proffered overshoes, they were given paper gloves to wear in case they had an urge to touch anything. It would be soon coming to the stage when all visitors to a locus would have to wear a full oversuit and perhaps breathing apparatus. When that day came, thought MacLeod, I leave.

They walked round to the rear of the hall and saw an ashen looking Constable Frank Nisbett, he asked for means of identification and when shown the warrant cards, he slammed to attention and saluted.

MacLeod visibly jumped at the stamp

of his feet, 'Careful, son. You may disturb the evidence.'

Nisbett looked a little abashed and relaxed, he blushed and opened the door for the detectives.

MacLeod led the way, he stopped at the entrance and took in the scene. He saw Sister Jenny, head to one side and a gaping hole in her neck, her eyes were open and seemed to look at him. She had an expression of pity on her face, as if she knew her attacker and was, even in the moment of death, forgiving him.

He looked round the room and walked to the table, he heard a disembodied voice say 'I've finished there it's okay.'

He looked round for the owner of the voice and saw a white-clad young girl appear from behind the table. She looked so very young.

He nodded and introduced himself and his team. 'Found anything?'

She replied, 'No, nothing actually, but we live in hope.' She picked up her bag and went through the door to the main hall.

Janet said, 'A bit rude these civvies, she

169

could have told us who she was.'

MacLeod looked through the desk, it appeared that someone had already rifled the contents.

Janet went to a picture of the Queen on the wall, she moved it and behind was a small safe, she tried the door and it was open. The safe was completely empty.

Janet sighed, 'Ah well, the murderer must have known about this too. She rarely locked it, said she couldn't remember numbers. She would only have had about thirty pounds in it and some papers. She drew the money from the local bank on a daily basis.'

'She didn't have a cash card then,' Susan remarked.

'She didn't like computers, she got it every night at closing time, it was a ritual. She was told not to be so predictable, she could have been robbed. Sister Jenny was a formidable woman and well liked, no one dared go near her.'

MacLeod said to Susan, 'We may be lucky, get to the bank and find out if she was given new notes. They may be able to tell us the numbers. We've got to get some

luck, we haven't had much up to now.'
Susan left immediately.

MacLeod and Janet stayed for a further
fifteen minutes quietly and carefully
examining everything without disturbing
too much. Janet quietly closed Sister
Jenny's eyelids, all photographs had been
taken, it seemed right. She said a quiet
prayer and then followed MacLeod out of
this place of death.

They met up at the car, Susan was
pleased with herself, Sister Jenny had
come into the bank as usual last night
and as she disliked used notes, and even
preferred pound notes, he had given her
thirty Bank of Scotland one pound notes
in pristine condition.

The morning had not been busy and
they had issued recycled notes this
morning. The teller had remembered that
Sister Jenny was in a hurry, she told him
she had an appointment and did not talk
as much as they normally did. She left in
a fluster.

He was distraught that Sister Jenny had
been so thoughtlessly murdered and
would be missed. He had already written

down the numbers of the notes, he was an intelligent youth, and if no one had come in by lunch time he would have rung the local police.

At last MacLeod thought to himself, something positive, he felt the gloom lift. He did not feel like calling into Pitt Street and update the ACC, he had a natural aversion to updating a senior officer when he didn't have anything to say. He preferred to get on with the job and update when necessary.

At the incident room, he was confronted by an agitated Detective Inspector Reade.

'You haven't had your mobile on.'

MacLeod looked at his phone, 'Whoops, sorry, what is it? It can't be that important Peter.'

'Oh yes, it is, your friend Joe Armstrong has been taken into hospital with a heart attack.'

'Joe always did over do it.'

Reade went on, 'And a message from HQ, Detective Superintendent Hamilton is too ill to take over the case and anyway he is being moved back to HQ once he gets better, Quality of Service I believe, and you are to take his place on this case as Acting Superintendent. It was felt that a new Detective Superintendent would take too long to get up to speed on the case.'

MacLeod sat down with a bump, it was the first time he had been 'acting up'. It made little difference to his pay, but it showed that he would be considered for the next rank after all.

Detective Inspector Janet MacBain said, 'Well, it's drinks all round then.'

'No, not until we get the bastard. What's to do Peter? We'll have a case conference as soon as we've finished.'

'We have two actions to do before we can really assess the facts.'

He turned to Janet MacBain and said, 'Could you see Helen MacDonald, the rest of the hen party have been seen and can't remember anything about last night. I thought it best a senior detective see her, you would be the best one.'

Janet grimaced, 'When?'

'I've made an appointment, all you do is ring and if she is in she will see you at

173

her home. It's only round the corner in Park Road.'

Reade then said to MacLeod, 'I've made an appointment for you and whoever you want to see the Americans at the Argyll at 3 p.m.'

'Right, Susan you and John will come with me, but I need a coffee now.' John Milton had the coffee ready and handed it to MacLeod, he knew his friend had little sleep and needed the caffeine boost.

MacLeod walked into his office and sat down. He was not thinking of the promotion, he was thinking that he should consider someone to act up in his place should this case go on much longer.

Peter Reade, he had complete faith in him as an Office Manager, he was firm and capable of making decisions in his absence. He was a very good plodding detective, but did not have the flashes of intuition which could make him a great detective. He was dependable and loyal and could work in the most trying of conditions. He kept the team working together and ensured every 't' was crossed and every 'i' was dotted. He had, at one

174

time, picked office managers from anyone who happened to be around, but soon discovered that the lynch pin of any case was the office man.

Detective Inspector Peter Reade was born to the job of office manager, he enjoyed it and showed his skill in every way, but was he capable of running a team? Could he be the DCI? MacLeod doubted it, but he had to think of the team's reaction if he did not put Reade in his chair.

He thought about Janet MacBain, she was certainly like him and could make DCI, but had she the experience? Once again he doubted it. If he was instructed to make one of them up, it had to be Reade, the team demanded it even if his own inclinations were to see how MacBain would perform in the job.

He suddenly had a vision of Helen MacDonald meeting Janet MacBain, he laughed out loud, these two strong women on a collision course. He put Janet as evens favourite to win. Helen had no idea what she was about to meet.

15

Detective Inspector Janet MacBain had heard about Helen MacDonald, she was not looking forward to the interview.

Janet rang the bell and within seconds Helen came to the door, 'Come in,' she boomed. That was the only word that could describe her tone.

Despite having a good night out, Helen showed none of the signs of wear and tear the other members of the hen party had shown. She was positively glowing. Janet followed her into a neat and tidy lounge, the outside of the house belied it's interior. A huge leather couch was facing the window, the view took in the hills behind Dunoon.

'That's why we bought it you know, I prefer to look at hills not the water, can't swim you know and I don't even like going on the ferry. I know what happened at the hotel, the other girls have been on the phone. It's a pity we didn't stay on.

My idea of heaven, interviewing a murderer after he had done the dastardly deed.'

Janet had not had time to get a word in as yet, she held up her hand for silence, 'Helen, I need to talk to you, can we have a cup of tea please?'

'Sorry, I'm not thinking, tea's already made when you rang.'

She turned to the table at the side of the television and poured out two cups.

Helen settled herself into a well worn armchair, 'Go ahead, I'm more used to asking the questions so bear with me. If I ask you anything I shouldn't know, please don't take offence.'

There was a gleam in her eyes as she said it. Janet would be asked as many questions as she asked.

This was an interesting few hours for both of them. The clash of the Titans. Anyone who had observed the civilised questions and answers would have missed the underlying tension of the strong-minded women, Janet would ask a question and Helen would reply with an innocuous answer, but with a question of her own. She was trying to get as much information from Janet about the case, as the other was trying to find out as much as she could about the evening Detective Superintendent Hamilton was attacked.

'Can you tell me what you saw during the time you were at the Argyll?'

'I don't remember a lot, I didn't see anyone in the bar. Was it really an Abercrombie, the body?'

'You should know, can we get back to the night, cast your mind back, really think.'

'Hmm, no we went in, saw Iris, had a couple of drinks. Was she really garrotted?'

'Couldn't say, what time did you leave?'

'About midnight, had to work you know. A bit like you, been back to Glasgow? Did you know this nun that was killed?'

'I don't know what you mean, can we stay with last night please.'

And so the interview proceeded.

The questions from Helen became more subtle, she realised she would not be able to rattle this lady.

The upshot was that really Helen could not tell Janet anything, she had not noticed anything at all, but they both gained respect for each other and in happier times there could be a firm friendship of equals.

Janet left the house feeling that she had just appeared before a promotion board, rarely did she have to be on her toes and been so expertly questioned. She knew she had given nothing away, but whilst walking the few minutes back to the station, she did mull over the conversation in her mind to make absolutely sure.

★ ★ ★

At 3 p.m. precisely, MacLeod accompanied by Detective Sergeant Susan Lampart and Detective Sergeant Milton, arrived at the Argyll Hotel.

Mrs White was, as usual, in the kitchen, she quickly appeared after being summoned by the receptionist, she was wiping her hands on her apron and looked a little harassed.

'Staff problems again, but we'll

manage, the Chambers are in the back lounge, I thought you may like a bit of privacy.'

She conducted them to the back of the hotel, she had put a 'Private' notice on the door and ushered them in. Mrs White did not stay, she was too busy to be curious.

They went into the room and saw the Chambers, they had a tray of coffee in front of them, there were six cups. Mrs Chambers said 'The coffee has just arrived, would you like some?' Both Milton and Lampart said 'Yes, please.' MacLeod declined the offer.

Mrs Chambers poured the coffee. After they had settled, Mr Chambers said, 'I gather there must be a problem, we were told about the attack on one of the guests, it's shocking especially here in Dunoon, you expect it in New York, but not here.'

Milton said, 'If you are worried about it I shouldn't be, we have had a murder and an attack in the last week, but I don't expect another for the next twenty years. The last one was so long ago we can't remember.'

MacLeod said, 'Yes, it's that kind of place, children can run free here without their parents worrying. Before we talk about last night, could I ask you some questions about your reasons for being here?'

'Reasons,' said Mrs Chambers, 'We are touring Europe, my husband has been ill and has retired early, we thought that a leisurely tour of Europe would be nice.'

MacLeod said to Mr Chambers, 'You said something about revisiting places, as you were in the Navy?'

'Yes, that was another lifetime ago, I was a young officer posted to the Holy Loch for a few months in the early sixties. I met Clara's brother there, he was tragically killed in an air crash on his way home.

It was through this I met Clara. I visited her father and there she was a fifteen year old troublemaker.'

He grinned at Clara and went on, 'We kept in contact and when I went back for a visit, she had grown up into the most beautiful woman I had ever seen, I wasn't about to let her go and we got engaged when she was eighteen, and married after I left law school, and we have been together ever since.'

He looked at Clara, it was obvious that he saw the beautiful young woman, not the middle aged plump but still attractive woman who sat beside him.

MacLeod said, 'Could you tell me what kind of vehicle you borrowed for the trip?'

'I got a Volvo, but when we got to Edinburgh I remembered the roads and went to Avis and swopped it for a Range Rover, they had to get it specially for me, can you imagine, a hire car firm in Scotland not having Range Rovers?'

'When did you arrive in Edinburgh, please?'

'About a week ago, we went up the east coast, and made our way down to Oban the night before last, then we came here.'

'Have you any proof of that, sir?'

'Proof, proof, why would we need that?'

'I'm afraid I must ask.'

Chambers was not at all put out, he had worked with the police long enough to know that they never asked without good reason, and that he would find out in good time why he was being asked.

Mrs Chambers interrupted and said, 'I have all the receipts in the room dear, shall I get them?'

MacLeod said, 'That would be ideal, would you go with Mrs Chambers and get them Sergeant Lampart?'

Susan looked up a little put out, she wanted to stay, but she would not dare argue. As she left MacLeod gave her a hard look and said, 'There's no rush.'

She realised she had a job to do, talking to Mrs Chambers and keeping her busy for a while.

As the women left the room MacLeod said, 'Did you hire a private detective to find a woman?'

'Yes, we did, we found him through the Greenock Police who recommended him to me. We came over for a few days last year, but we stayed in Glasgow and only did a short trip, enough to give Joe Armstrong the facts. I wanted to find the girl, I felt so guilty about it all, I still do. I'm pleased you didn't talk about it in front of her.'

MacLeod said, 'I realised that as soon

as you didn't mention it, but why?'

'Dave's father made a dying wish for Clara to find this girl, I tried to talk her out of it, but she can be stubborn at times and I gave in and hired a private detective.'

'She knew I was here in the Navy, but in all these years I didn't tell her about her brother, her father told her that he had a relationship with a woman here. Clara believes that her brother was a saint but I know different and I don't want her to be disillusioned.'

'Dave was different to me and Clara. He was wild and was a lot of fun to be with, but mostly irresponsible. He met a young woman, he didn't tell me who she was but she was 'classy' as he put it.'

'Well, I saw him fall in love, I only saw him once with her, she was beautiful and they were besotted with each other. Then Dave was on his way home and killed.'

'He had been to the CO to ask permission to marry her, he was on his way before he had finished talking to the CO.'

Chambers paused. He had a far away look in his eyes.

MacLeod waited and after a short time Chambers continued, 'Well, I tried to find out who this girl was, Dave had met her in Dunoon somewhere. I thought she was a local tart, but Dave insisted she wasn't.

'If this girl was a tart it would taint his memory, if she is found and is a nice lady it would upset Clara that her father got him on the plane that caused his death, either way I lose.

'Clara will be disappointed in either her father or her brother, and as I was here at the time and told her nothing about this affair from when we first met she may blame me. I'm on a hiding to nothing. I want nothing to come between Clara and me.'

Chambers shrugged his shoulders and said in a brisker tone, 'We have had regular updates from Joe Armstrong, and a month ago he sent a report telling us that he had found her, fortunately I intercepted this one, he wanted to go and see her, but I said no. It seems that the affair she had with Dave caused her to have a very unhappy life. I can't tell Clara. I was hoping to see Joe tomorrow to tell him to forget everything and sort out a report for Clara that will keep the memory of her father and brother intact. Could we please change the subject when my wife returns?'

'I'm sorry to tell you this, Joe Armstrong has been taken into hospital with a mild heart attack, I rang them today and he can have visitors but has to stay in for a couple of days.

'The other piece of bad news, I'm afraid the woman you were seeking is dead, she was murdered three days ago.'

Chambers looked at MacLeod with widening eyes, 'And you think we may have something to do with it?'

Chambers was no fool.

MacLeod said, 'It was a passing thought, you will agree that you have a good motive. We must check every detail of your alibi.'

He smiled and said, 'But I wouldn't worry, you may be able to kill, but it wasn't you I saw at the window, your shadow is too big.'

MacLeod knew this man could take a comment like this without offence.

Chambers said, 'Maybe, but I could have hired someone.'

MacLeod and Milton both burst out laughing. 'Not in this town,' Milton said, 'You couldn't hire a man to clean your windows without anyone knowing.'

'That's as maybe but I think I will brush up on my Scots Law. Do I really need to tell you that we had nothing to do with it?'

When Mrs Chambers and Susan returned from the room, MacLeod thanked them for their time and as they left he paid his bill at the reception for the previous few days. He looked at the bill as he was walking out and said to his staff, 'Excuse me a moment.'

He went back to the receptionist and queried something. He had a look of dawning comprehension. Whilst walking to the car Susan showed MacLeod a wad of receipts in her hand.

'Mrs Chambers keeps everything, all neat and tidy in a small mobile office file. I wish I was that organised.'

He didn't seem to hear her and as she was about to say something else, John put his hand on her arm and shook his head, she became quiet.

They arrived back at the police office and MacLeod said, 'Conference now. The DIs and DSs.'

* * *

Detective Inspectors MacBain and Reade, Detective Sergeants Lampart and Milton sat in MacLeod's office, it was a little cramped. MacLeod said, 'Have you checked the alibi's of Doctor Lamont's husband, Peter?'

'Yes, they were both together when Mary was murdered, she had to get up early to go to Glasgow.'

'So that means they have given an alibi for each other, any witnesses?'

'Of course not,' said Reade, 'they were in bed.'

'He didn't have an alibi when Hamilton was attacked, Muriel was the duty doctor at the Cottage Hospital, she gave him emergency treatment. What kind of cars do they have?'

'One is a Range Rover and the other is

a Volvo Estate, we haven't got round to checking theirs, we haven't had enough staff to get through the list yet.'

'What's this all about, guv?' said Milton.

'Two things really. I told Chambers that you couldn't do anything in this town without someone knowing and it's strange no one saw anything out of the ordinary.'

MacBain said, 'Unless they saw something that wasn't out of the ordinary, someone who is seen and it doesn't register.'

Lampart said, 'Like a vet going on a call out.' Reade, ever the sceptic, said, 'It can't be, he doesn't have a motive.'

'Yes, he does,' said MacLeod, 'I would have thought that about two million pounds would be motive enough.'

'Of course, they spent more than two hundred and fifty thousand on the laboratory at the back of their home. If Mary had turned up, the presumption of death would have been overturned and she may have inherited, lock stock and barrel.' Reade could be quick when he wanted to be.

'But she only had six months to live,' said Lampart. 'That six months could have made all the difference, she could have made someone else her heir and he would have lost his practice, he depends on his wife's money to continue,' said Milton.

Reade said, 'Can you tell me exactly how you have come to this conclusion, it's going to take some bottle to go after him. There's no evidence.'

MacLeod carefully put his hotel bill on the desk, he said, 'Innellan five-six-seven-two.' They were startled out of their slouching over the desks.

Reade looked at the number. 'How on earth . . . ' he began.

MacLeod interrupted, 'This is the second thing. I saw the receptionist, she told me that six months ago the numbers were changed, but everyone round here ignores the longer number and still uses the old ones, it's going to take some years for them to change. This is their private number and Morris would only have access to ex-directory numbers through the operator and she would not have looked for the last four numbers. Muriel Lamont rang the first night we were in the hotel and put the call on my bill.'

'I still can't believe it, the murders are so . . . so ghoulish, anyway he couldn't have known Sister Jenny,' said Reade.

'Maybe he didn't but she could,' commented MacBain 'I know the homeless are looked after by volunteer doctors, it's organised by the Church on a rota system, they visit on a Thursday and any dosser who wants a check up goes to the hall in the afternoon. I'll get on and check, after this.'

She was visibly excited, she felt that they were getting somewhere at last. Reade held up his hand and said, 'All right, so Doctor Lamont could have known her, what's the motive?'

MacBain looked down as she answered, Reade was a little obtuse at times, 'Muriel could have found out who Mary really was, she told her husband it's not unknown you know.'

Reade looked a little uncomfortable. MacBain went on, 'He may have believed that Sister Jenny could have known too. Mary may have told her and after all we knew who she was, he may have been clearing up any loose ends.'

MacLeod said, 'That's enough speculation, we have to get everything checked again, but be careful, no one is to mention names or it could be blown, if we ask they will be told, now sort out the ones we need to re-visit. Tell the rest of the team nothing. This is for us and no one else.'

Reade conceded, 'Okay, I'll go with the motive for Sister Jenny, but what about Mr Hamilton?'

MacLeod said, 'We will find that one out when we speak to him, my crystal ball is a little cloudy at the moment.'

Lampart made her own contribution to the discussion, 'I can't believe that his wife could be a murderer, she saves life, not takes it, she is so gentle. I can't believe she knows anything about this.'

MacBain said 'I don't think we should discount her as a potential suspect. That kind of money is a great incentive. It could be the other way round, she could be the perpetrator and he knows nothing about it.'

MacLeod was pleased with MacBain, she was showing that she was thinking, using her detective intuition but was a little impatient with Reade, he wanted all the answers before they had the questions or any of the facts. He said, 'I will go to the Inverclyde, I want to find out how Mr Hamilton is getting on, I'll visit Joe when I am there, ring me if you get anything. Don't update anyone except me and that includes force headquarters.

'I'll visit the Fiscal on my way to the ferry. He will be pleased we have someone in the frame, he is a very good friend of John Lamont. I must tell him or he will be very upset if I don't, get your coat John, we are off again.'

He didn't have to say that the Fiscal would keep his mouth shut, it was more than his job's worth to say anything. The team needed to eliminate one or the other of the Lamonts before taking this investigation further, but both had to be suspects for now.

16

MacLeod and Milton walked into the Fiscal's office. MacLeod felt a little apprehensive, Grey would not be pleased at this update. Maureen Stewart was at her desk, she looked up at him, her eyes were slightly bloodshot and she seemed weary.

'If you go out at night, you should remember we are not as young as we used to be.'

'Do I look that bad, I thought I wasn't showing it. Anyway how do you feel, I heard you had a hard night too?'

'Well enough.'

He was taken aback, he had a flash back, and saw Hamilton on the bed in the dark, heard the hollow rasp of his breath as he held his neck, his life ebbing away with his strength.

The silhouette at the window loomed in his mind. MacLeod shook his head to get rid of this unwanted intrusion, it disturbed him.

'Are you all right, Cameron?' Maureen became anxious, she saw that MacLeod's face had drained and he looked unwell.

'I'm fine, I think I need a good night's sleep. Could I see the Fiscal now? John, keep Maureen company, I'm sure she will get you a cup of coffee.'

Grey listened with a sinking heart to the story MacLeod had to tell, he was saddened and angry at the same time. MacLeod didn't take long.

'Why do you think John is the murderer?'

'Until I got the telephone number he wasn't in the frame, and everything seems to have fallen into place. He's a vet and these people were butchered like animals.'

'Yes, he is a vet, not a butcher, he saves the lives of animals, he only kills when necessary. I've known him for three years. I can't believe it, really I can't.'

'If that's the case, the two alternatives are, one, they are working together, or two, Muriel is a serial killer, she is fit and healthy, she strikes me that she has taken good care of herself. She gives me the impression of a cat, all soft fur but with an underlying curled up strength. I wouldn't like to cross her.'

'I can't believe that either of them are capable of murder.'

'You are an expert on John, I haven't seen him yet. On the other hand I saw Muriel at the hospital last night. She did a great job and worked like a demon to save him. Perhaps I'm barking up the wrong tree.'

'What about the Americans, are they possible?'

'The receipts for the hotels seem to clear them. The hotels are being contacted now, but the night Mary died they were in Inverness, and the day Sister Jenny was murdered they were in Fort William. The night Hamilton nearly died they were in the Argyll, but they didn't have a motive, nor do the Lamonts. I cannot understand this one.'

MacLeod became silent and Grey knew this man, he couldn't lie very well and there was something else he hadn't been told.

'What are you keeping back, Cameron?'

MacLeod thought for a while and decided that he was about to break a confidence, something he had never done before and he hoped never to do it again, but in the circumstances he had to tell Grey. He took a deep breath as if he were trying to overcome a silent barrier within himself.

'Hamilton told me that he was adopted and was born on the same day as Mary's child, he was worried that he may be her son. We are getting the information through soon, exactly where Mary's children are, and who adopted them.'

MacLeod stopped and became agitated, 'Oh, shit! Muriel Lamont. She was outside my door when he told me, perhaps she overheard. The will says the child inherits even if it had been adopted. If he were Mary's offspring there is a great motive. It must be, we can't find any other reason for this.'

'You will have to get your security tightened in future Cameron, it seems there's been a modicum of laxity.'

Grey saw the stricken look on MacLeod's face and decided that his friend needed some reassurance. 'It could happen to anyone, Cameron. Now we have a motive for the attack on Hamilton, make sure he is guarded day and night, I don't want a successful assault. It wouldn't do to have a senior police officer murdered. Public confidence is low already, to have another death would be, how shall I say it. It would make me very unhappy, Mr MacLeod.'

MacLeod took the Fiscal's point, he didn't want another death to complicate the issue, he took it personally that Sister Jenny had been murdered, he felt somehow responsible for not ensuring her safety. A completely illogical thought, but she was a witness in the case and he had failed to ensure her safety.

'He is being guarded day and night. He hasn't been able to speak yet but he is being allowed family visits. I'm hoping to see him soon, he may be able to help us.'

'It's no good pushing it, I want a live witness not a dead one please. Now I don't think you have enough evidence to arrest these two. A telephone number is hardly enough, when you get some hard evidence then we'll discuss it, they haven't run away up to now so don't see them until we are ready. On the other hand you could clear them and we are back to square one.'

Grey was secretly hoping the latter would be the case, he liked John Lamont, they were in the local Rotary Club and had spent many a good night together.

MacLeod had a bad feeling as he left Grey's office, he now had two suspects, he knew that one of them was the murderer and a psychopath, and perhaps the other was co-conspirator. He felt that until one or both of them were locked away he would not feel entirely confident there would not be another murder.

This murderer was clever, resourceful and dedicated to self-preservation, but which one was it or both, he was hoping to find out soon.

He left the Fiscal's office and saw Milton was leaning on the counter, he was in the middle of an animated conversation with Maureen, he heard her say, 'Never again, next time they can celebrate on their own.'

'Never again until the next time.' said MacLeod.

Milton looked up and saw MacLeod tapping his fingers on the counter. 'Where to now, guv?'

'The Inverclyde, we are doing welfare visits.'

The drive to the ferry took a few minutes, MacLeod was pensive and worried, he was missing something. On the ferry he remembered.

'John, have we found the Galloping Major yet?'

'No, he hasn't turned up, I know we are still looking for him.'

'Drop me off at the Inverclyde and go round to Greenock Police Station, get the search for him hurried up. If Sister Jenny was murdered in case she knew anything, perhaps the murderer saw our reluctant witness at the railway station. He may not know anything but the perp is unlikely to know that, I don't want another corpse on our hands.'

'What if he won't come to the station?'

'I'm sure he can be persuaded, all I want is him found, alive and in one piece. I'll ring you when I'm ready to be picked up.'

MacLeod was dropped off at the top of the hill at the entrance to the hospital. The Inverclyde Hospital is a modern high rise building, indistinguishable from other modern hospitals throughout the country. The NHS had found an architect who had not got out of childishly playing with building blocks and brought that to his work. It is all glass and confusion. There's a reception desk, but rarely manned due to the cuts.

Signs are carefully placed so that out patients and visitors can find their way about. X-ray, a popular destination is found by following the blue line embedded in the floor, Pathology could be found by following the red line and so on. Hospital floors reminded MacLeod of the yellow brick road.

He had to force his way past a group of smokers in the foyer. Smoking was not allowed in the hospital, MacLeod was always amused that a confirmed smoker could go to hospital for a minor operation or tests, not the most calming of situations and be forced to temporarily give up smoking. They had to suffer from the stress of their illness and the added stress of nicotine deprivation.

Some experts in the field of addiction said that it was easier for some to give up heroin than smoking and yet the 'caring' profession had all the sympathy in the world for the heroin sufferer and gave a substitute, yet a smoker was on his or her own with the withdrawal symptoms.

He smoked cigars occasionally now, he had struggled for years to give up the weed. He hated the New Puritans who cared for others' physical appearance, at least the Old Puritans cared about others' souls, they didn't have the modern media to proclaim their brand of philosophy.

He suddenly had a thought and said to himself, 'I haven't been bombarded as much by the New Puritans, they must be doing something else now. Perhaps animal rights and the state of the earth. I hope so, I've seen too many relatively young men die through taking up strenuous activities to get fit. I don't want to be a healthy corpse.'

MacLeod got to the ward, and approached the central desk. It was a deserted desk, all the nurses that passed them were in a hurry and obviously were preoccupied with their work, it proved impossible to attract their attention. He gave up and walked down the ward, on looking into one, saw a uniformed police officer sitting reading a book.

He went in, the constable looked up and recognised MacLeod, he stood up. MacLeod waived to him to sit down.

MacLeod looked behind a curtain, Hamilton was lying on his back on a white hospital bed, he had a drip in his right arm attached to a blood bag on a stand, his neck was bandaged and a tube was attached to his throat. He appeared asleep. As MacLeod approached the bed the door opened and he felt a hand on his shoulder, and when he turned he saw a nurse standing behind him. She put a finger to her lips to indicate he should keep quiet and nodded towards the door. He was being unceremoniously, but quietly ejected.

'What are you doing in here?' she had that imperious tone of the One In Charge.

'I couldn't get anyone's attention.'

MacLeod introduced himself and quickly produced his warrant card from his shirt pocket. She relaxed a little but went on firmly, 'He can only have family as visitors, he can't speak and we don't want him disturbed. His vocal chords were nicked and he is under mild sedation in case he is tempted to try, we don't want further damage.'

'When will he be ready to be seen, I won't let him speak, but we need to know what he saw.'

MacLeod looked at the nurse, under his gaze she became very uncomfortable and finally she spoke, 'I'll see the doctor, but he can't be seen today, perhaps tomorrow. Ring back sometime then.'

As MacLeod was moving away from the door, he saw an elderly woman approach. She was in her sixties, small and walked with a straight back which made her look taller, she was wearing the dress of a countrywoman, tweed skirt, cashmere sweater, tweed jacket. Her hair was cut fairly short, but it was a mass of unruly curls, tinged with black over grey. She had an anxious look on her face.

The nurse looked at her with recognition, 'Here again, Mrs Hamilton. He's doing fine, now don't stay too long today.'

'I won't, but I need to be near my boy.'

MacLeod was amused at the description of Hamilton, he would be mortified at the description, after all he was a high ranking officer. MacLeod briefly thought about his own mother who died many years ago. She always called him my boy, even when he was certainly and obviously not a boy.

'Excuse me Mrs Hamilton, may I have a word?'

Mrs Edwina Hamilton turned with pale blue eyes on this stranger, she had a pleasant open face and was not averse to talking to strangers. 'Of course, young man, what can I do for you?'

MacLeod introduced himself and asked the nurse if they could use a private office. The blue clad nurse showed them to a small room at the end of the ward.

'I'm sorry to ask you this, Mrs Hamilton, but we really need to know something which is very private, I assure you I will be the only one to know.

Mrs Hamilton was intrigued, there were no secrets in her past, she couldn't imagine what it was. 'Go on, I don't have any secrets.'

'Could you tell me where you adopted your son?'

Mrs Hamilton was taken aback, she didn't expect this.

'Adopted my son, yes, I can remember it as if it were yesterday. We hadn't been able to have children, it isn't as now you know, there was little treatment for couples like us. Well, a young cousin of ours became pregnant, all the family knew we wanted a child so desperately.'

She paused, she thinking of the trauma of wanting a child so desperately and not being able to be a complete family, the false hopes to be always dashed.

'Her parents were horrified and she wanted to keep the baby. The father was a little feckless, a trait of youth, I'm afraid.

She was sent to Newcastle to relatives to have the baby. She had a very bad time and in the cold light of day, when the practicalities of rearing a child appeared she became less enthusiastic about it.'

'With the family's agreement I looked after my boy from birth and we got together with the social workers and we adopted him. Had to be legal you know. We decided not to tell him who his mother really was, after all he knows her, and the family thought it best not to complicate things. Is that all you need to know?'

'Where is his mother now?'

'She went to London and has made a good life for herself, an important executive with a bank you know. She did marry but divorced, she had two more children. We see her now and again, but we don't mention it.'

'Yes, I'm very grateful, you have put my mind at rest. Don't you think he should know, he can trace his biological parents now, the law says so.'

'I know. We have thought about it, but the subject hasn't come up. But it's not for you to tell him. Why do you need to know anyway?'

'I think I'll leave it up to him to tell you, when he can speak that is. I'm sure he will ask you now. Thank you for your time. No one else will know about our conversation.'

Mrs Hamilton went to the small hospital room where her son lay she was a little disturbed at the conversation with MacLeod, however she was also a strong woman and lived in the present, anything that happened in the future was another thing, she faced problems as they arose and didn't spend energy worrying about what she could not change.

MacLeod decided he had time to see Joe, fortunately the coronary care ward was close. He saw Joe sitting on his bed, he was talking to a young nurse who was giggling and he heard her say, 'You can't do that. I've told you Mr Armstrong.'

MacLeod approached and Joe looked up at him, 'Well, I didn't expect to see you, Cameron. Welfare visit or something more sinister?'

The young nurse turned to MacLeod,

she looked so young that MacLeod was shocked, she couldn't be much older than his daughters. That's the sign of age, he thought, when nurses look young, never mind policemen.

'No Joe, just a visit from a friend. How on earth did you get in here? I thought you were looking after yourself.'

'Bad luck really, it's a good job I have been looking after myself and doing what the doctors have told me or you would have visited me in the morgue. I went back to the office and someone had broken in, my file on Mary Abercrombie has been stolen, I hope you took a complete copy or I'm sunk.'

'Of course I did, everything seemed important to the case, have you reported the break in?'

'Not yet, I had this little hiccup before I had time, anyway I thought it may have something to do with your case nothing else has gone. An amateurish break in too, I noticed straight way. Maybe you want to keep this to yourself so I thought I would contact you first.'

'Thanks Joe, I owe you one.'

'One, what do you mean one, I'll put it on the list.'

MacLeod and Armstrong spent a happy few hours reminiscing about their mutual past, Joe seemed cheered up when it came time to leave. As MacLeod got up, Joe became serious. 'Cameron, have you anyone in the 'frame' for this murder?'

'Nothing I can talk about, why?'

'If you do get a suspect, maybe I could help you. I worked here for the last ten years of my service, you know.'

'I'll keep that in mind, thanks.'

MacLeod left, to find a telephone to ring Milton to come and collect him, he had left the handset in the car again.

He must invent a phone that gave out a bleep every time he left it lying around. Perhaps that was an idea to play with, he may make money out of it, certainly more than anything he could make in the police force.

17

Detective Constable Frank Morris was feeling dejected. He had spent considerable time and effort in trying to identify the meaning of the four figure number found in the Duchess' coat pocket and the boss had solved the problem by paying his hotel bill.

It was so unfair, he thought a little self-pityingly. 'If I had asked the operator for ex-directory numbers it would have been solved within hours, now why didn't I think of that?' He enjoyed operating the computer and now he felt he was useless.

Morris was sitting at his desk in the incident room doodling on a pad, his glasses had slipped down his nose, making him look young and vulnerable. Suddenly his reverie was disturbed. Detective Inspector Reade came into the room. 'Snap out of it Morris, you can't be perfect all the time.'

'It isn't that, sir, computers can help a

great deal and I was hoping to show the boss how good they can be.'

'Morris, no amount of computers can overcome the main attribute for a good detective.'

'What's that, perseverance?'

'No, stop reading so many books. Luck my boy, sheer unadulterated luck, and the boss has it to overflowing. I could tell you stories about him.

'When he was in uniform he was banned from leaving the station to get his paperwork done, he had so many arrests. He went to the canteen in another building and as he was walking along the road he stopped a bloke. Bingo! Another arrest, he had just screwed a jewellers. That's what a detective needs luck.'

Morris tried to look a little enthusiastic, but if all you needed was luck he had better get back to uniform. His luck was so bad he had never even got a pound on a Lottery scratchcard, everyone else he knew had at least that.

'But I try and seem to get nowhere. I think I'm in the wrong job.'

'Listen, you and I will never have that

kind of luck. We would have gone to the canteen either minutes before or minutes after the boss, so we would have missed a good collar. We have to concentrate on our strengths so get on with yours, use the computer, show him what you can do.'

Reade regarded computers as ideal instruments to store his administration, he knew enough to appreciate their help in that field, but he had his doubts that they had any other uses. He was humouring Morris, he had to keep him occupied, Reade lived by the maxim that idle hands make work for the devil. He liked to see everyone busy, whether the work was useful or not.

Morris felt better, Detective Inspector Reade was nit picking at times but he knew what to say to a junior officer who was feeling down. Morris thought about the last meeting the supervisors had. Usually the whole team knew what was going on, this time was different which was a little strange, they hadn't told the rest what was going on.

Detective Inspector MacBain and

Detective Sergeant Lampart had gone out to the local council offices to 'check some details', or so they said as they left. He was not to be trusted with whatever they were doing.

Then Detective Constable Rod Mac-Pherson had been told to recheck the Lamonts' alibis, Rod had let it slip that he was not to tell anyone what he was doing.

Although he was not specifically told, he knew that the Lamonts were now suspects in the case.

Morris was feeling a little put out that he had been left to get on with the office tasks. He had traced the whereabouts of the children of Mary Abercrombie but now no one seemed interested. The eldest was an engineer in the Middle East and was actually out there for the last two months. He was married with three children. His adoptive parents had not told him about him being adopted.

He had spoken to the mother on the telephone and she was completely distraught if they should tell him. The two children of the man called Jimmy Bland were not so fortunate. The eldest died in a road accident at the age of seven. He had not been adopted and spent his short life in a children's home. The youngest child, a girl, had been adopted and she had married at the age of seventeen, divorced at twenty, with two children of her own. She was living in Greenock, so close to where her mother had been found. Her only means of support was Social Security. Her adoptive parents were both dead and he rang her himself. He spoke to a pleasant woman who was eager to please especially when he purported to be a social worker. It was obvious that she was unaware she was adopted from the telephone conversation and Morris took the decision, rightly, that she should not be contacted again. Reade confirmed his decision. Rather quickly Morris thought, it was as if he was preoccupied elsewhere.

The last child of Mary was a businessman in Glasgow. When Morris rang his parents home, he answered and it was fortunate he knew of his adoption, Morris mistook the man for his adoptive father.

Although the man had known he was adopted, he had never had the inclination to trace his biological mother. Morris thought that now was not the time to tell him that his real mother had been washed up on the banks of the Clyde as if she were so much flotsam.

Morris apologised for his mistake, he identified himself as a research worker for a psychiatrist writing a book on adoption, and said that this case would not be of interest to his principal as he was looking for those adoptees who had traced or attempted to trace their biological parents. He seemed quite happy with the explanation.

Thus Morris had cleared any of Mary's children of suspicion. He felt he had nothing else to do and no one seemed very interested in his results, it was as if he had wasted his time in tracing the kids. It was in this mood that Reade found him.

Morris was determined to shine, somehow, he had been always the best man, never the groom. No matter what he had contributed to a case, someone else seemed to get the glory. Morris thought about the case, he considered the options and, without the aid of his computer he came to the conclusion that the Lamonts were the prime suspects. He turned to his computer screen, and brought up his own programs. He used a computer and modem as an artist used paint. He was a master, he was probably the only one who didn't know it.

Morris worked with great concentration. So much so he did not hear Reade leave the room to go downstairs to see Sergeant Gillespie. He did not hear the telephone, nor did he hear the rest of the team return.

His friend and colleague, Rod MacPherson, stopped the others from disturbing him. He knew when Frank was working well, he was not swearing at his inanimate computer as if it were a feeling person, he was plugged in and the computer became almost an extension of him.

Suddenly Morris looked up, his eyes were glazed, 'They did it, and I can prove it.'

'How, not with that thing I hope.'

Detective Sergeant Lampart was wary about computers, she mistrusted them and would always print out information, she liked the feel of paper, it felt right somehow. She may have used a computer to get it, but was not confident until she saw it in black and white on something she could hold.

Janet MacBain was more pragmatic, 'Prove what, Frank?'

'They murdered the old lady.'

'Frank, Mary Abercrombie was not an old lady, just because she had lived past fifty, she was not old.'

'No I don't mean her, I mean the old lady, the aunt.'

There was a horrified silence in the room. The atmosphere could have been cut with a knife, the whole team seemed frozen in time, all looked at him. Detective Inspector Reade broke the silence.

'Not another murder, haven't we got enough with The Duchess, Sister Jenny and the attempt on Mr Hamilton?'

Detective Constable MacPherson trusted

his partner's instincts, he knew when something important was about to be said.

'Okay, explain.'

Morris cleared his throat, he looked towards the little group clustered around him, but his eyes were unfocused and he gave his report quickly as if he needed to talk without interruption, as if he needed to speak or the knowledge would fly from his mind.

'I thought that I should check the Lamonts' background a little deeper, well I found the report of the old Aunt's death. The death certificate said she died of an embolism you know. I didn't really know what that was so I checked. It is an obstruction of a blood vessel by any foreign substance, a blood clot or a fat globule from a broken limb or an air bubble. I can't pronounce the words,' Reade was about to interrupt to tell Morris to get on with it, but MacBain held up her hand and he stopped, 'but one in the brain can prove fatal. I looked back at the post-mortem results and it seemed a little odd, no foreign body in the blood vessels to cause the blockage, but she had signs of an embolism in the brain, it could have been caused by anything.

'The pathologist was veering on the side of a suspicious death but changed his mind. Well, he was about to retire and as she died at home in bed alone and was found by the housekeeper in the morning and no one had visited, he put it down to natural causes.'

Morris could be a little long winded and sometimes talked to himself rather than at an audience, it was as if he were clearing his thoughts by talking out loud. It was the longest speech any of the team had heard him speak.

'I checked Charing Cross Hospital, Doctor Lamont was on leave the day before her aunt died and the day after. They keep wonderful records, their administration is very good. I couldn't check John Lamont's whereabouts without speaking to him. His old practice had a computer but I couldn't get into it. I hate stand alone computers, you can't get into them without everyone knowing, you have to have a modem and be connected.'

He looked up and saw signs of irritation on Reade's face, he would have explained further about the disadvantages of stand alone computers to a searcher such as he, but changed his mind. 'They came here and killed her, up one day, back the next.'

'What are you talking about Morris, killed her, came up one day and back the next, there's no facts.' Reade was now getting very annoyed.

'Oh, didn't I tell you, Muriel Lamont was given a speeding ticket on the M74 in Dumfries the same night her Aunt died, she was doing eighty-five going north at 8.10 p.m. The ticket didn't say how many passengers there were. I don't expect they took the children, they probably left them at home with a babysitter or with friends.'

'They could have been anywhere, they could go anywhere from the M74.' Reade, ever the sceptic would not admit there could be anything in this sort of speculation.

'I don't think so, the local police went

to their house about midday the following day, after the old Aunt had been found dead, they were both there and they said they had been at home all night. I've got access to the file, for some reason a statement was asked for. Did you know that Joe Armstrong asked for the statement, it was just before he retired from the force, he could have been a little suspicious too. Unusual asking for statements about the whereabouts of the next of kin, don't you think?'

'What made you look for this?'

'I don't know, if they were prepared to kill to keep the money, I thought they might kill to get it in the first place.'

Rod MacPherson was proud of his partner, sometimes he was put down because of his appearance and he knew he was the best one he had ever had, he was always pleased when Frank came through, but this was something else, he had really excelled himself and he knew in his bones that Frank was right.

Janet MacBain was delighted with this information, she felt the same as MacPherson they had them. They could pick up Lamonts and legitimately question them, what came out of the interviews would be the end of the case. This was hard evidence, not merely a simple number.

'Get the copy of the ticket; get everything you can Frank, we need to have it all before the DCI comes back. We can put it to him then get them in. Let's get as much as we can.'

Susan Lampart was listening intently to everything that was said, she was becoming more convinced of the guilt of the Lamonts. She was now convinced they were working together in this, and it was time Morris and MacPherson were informed of the suspicions, not that they needed any telling, they had worked it out for themselves.

'We had a good result at the Regional Health offices, Doctor Lamont does do a clinic when asked for, she is a volunteer but only when the regular doctors are sick, she was in Glasgow last week, just before the Duchess announced her good fortune to all and sundry, perhaps Mary was having one of her turns and looking for her children, it is a bit of a coincidence. Muriel could have put two and two together, and come up with four.'

'They would never have recognised each other, after all they hadn't seen much of each other when they were children so the chances of recognition now would have been remote.'

The team now had a purpose, they sorted out as much information as they could, put it in two files and laid them on the desk.

Reade worked out the timings for each murder and the alleged whereabouts of both accused. It was tight, but possible for both of them to be at the locus. He looked at his chart, he was pensive. Were they barking up the wrong tree, he hoped not. He was not as convinced as the others of their guilt.

Reade said to the team, 'Are we ready?' He looked around the room and received nods, 'All right then, I'll ring the boss and get him back here.'

18

MacLeod got into the car, Milton was unusually quiet, suddenly he broke the silence. 'The Galloping Major has been found, you aren't going to like it.'

'Alive I hope.'

'Yes, he's been in the Southern General Hospital for the last few days, suffering from alcoholic poisoning. He isn't very well.'

'Thank goodness he isn't dead. Why haven't we been told before?'

Milton thought about it for a while, he said with a sigh, 'When we sent out an all points, no one thought about checking the hospital.'

MacLeod was not surprised, in his day whenever an all points circular check was done, the hospitals nearest the police stations were automatically contacted. Now it seems that the same amount of care was not taken, and pride in the job was becoming a thing of the past.

Things are changing all over, he had friends in all walks of life, and the same universal complaint was made. MacLeod secretly felt that he and his friends were merely getting old, he remembered the old timers in his youth saying the same thing, but he felt that standards were slipping. 'How were we told then?'

'Someone gave him a bottle of whiskey, but had substituted one hundred percent alcohol. Dangerous stuff, and not easily obtained, only hospitals and laboratories are able to get it. He is very ill, they decided to test the bottle, he hadn't drunk it all and they found it. They rang the local police.'

MacLeod mentally changed his mind about standards and thanked the Lord there were some bright sparks left in the world.

'We'll have to check sources in the Glasgow area but we will probably find too many to be sure where the poison came from, I'll bet it came from Innellan, don't suppose I'll have any takers.'

He told Milton to drive to the Southern General, they went through

Greenock, past Port Glasgow. MacLeod noted that the old dark and forbidding flats adjacent to the road had been refurbished. They looked cleaner and welcoming, he couldn't see the inside but he hoped that the families that were forced to live in these tenements were better off than their predecessors and care had been taken to give them a better standard of surroundings.

He remembered when Port Glasgow was known as 'Indian Country', when police officers went in threes. Two to do the enquiry and one to look after the car. He made a trivial mental note to ask if it were the same now. He was always curious which was his great strength.

They had driven up the M8, the tide was out and the channel markers were standing proud from the mud flats, these stone markers were topped by lights, no boat was traversing the deep channel to the Clyde estuary. In the distant past the Clyde was one of the busiest of waterways, the noise from the shipyards was a background fanfare to the passage of the small, medium and large boats traversing the Clyde.

Now the river was quiet, no noise, no boats, no work. Dumbarton Rock at the other side of the river stood proud, the rock castle clinging precariously to the granite base.

As they were passing Glasgow Airport to the turning for Irvine the telephone rang. MacLeod answered. He listened and said, 'We will be back as soon as we can, don't do anything until we get back. Don't talk about it or do anything else,' and switched the phone off.

MacLeod turned to Milton, he was grinning broadly.

'Got them, young Morris has come up trumps with that computer, he can prove that Muriel Lamont could have murdered her aunt, she was given a speeding ticket on the way up. Gave a statement saying she was at home in Surrey when her Aunt died. Joe Armstrong was suspicious too, he got the Surrey police to get the statements from them. Good old Joe, always the careful one.'

Milton couldn't reply, he was in the

outside lane manoeuvring through heavy traffic, he had to concentrate. Scottish drivers in these parts know where they are going and tend not to tell anyone else, they forget to use their indicators as they expect everyone else to know where they are going too.

At the junction of the turn off for Hillington when the traffic eased he had time to reply, 'Morris has proved they could have killed the old aunt. That should be interesting, shall we go straight back?'

'No, let's see The Galloping Major first, he may be able to help prove they did Mary and Sister Jenny too.'

They arrived at the Southern General, an old workhouse converted to a hospital, as most of the old workhouses were, bits were added when the need arose, it sprawled over a considerable area.

Older parts were overshadowed by newer high rise office type buildings. A pedestrian walkway, enclosed in glass high above the main hospital road connected one side of the hospital to the other. Milton looked at it and made a mental note not to use it, it didn't seem too safe.

Finding a parking space in this mini town was tricky, eventually Milton found a space at the back of the Outpatients Department.

They went to the office of the local Unit Beat Policeman, Constable Cleary, and were lucky to find him. He escorted them to the right ward where the Galloping Major was at present being well looked after.

Cleary was a chatty older officer, he never hurried, and was proud of his job in the hospital. Whilst walking to the ward, to Milton's horror he took them over the walkway, he chatted about his work and his problems. He was proud of his work and the impact he had on vandalism and crime. He talked about the history of the hospital and said he was going to start a museum of sorts when he got the time.

The irony was that the Galloping Major was the type of person who would have been housed in this old workhouse in the distant past, now he was in the building to be cured and thrown back on the streets.

MacLeod thought about this, the Victorians took the poor in because they didn't like to see them on the streets, maybe now there should be some thought to setting up a similar system for humanitarian purposes, but not called a workhouse.

His own grandmother refused to come to this hospital because she remembered it as the workhouse, he remembered she shivered with fear at the mere suggestion.

They walked into the ward and saw a constable from the local station standing outside a small side room, as they approached MacLeod was bemused why he should be standing outside the room.

'What are you doing out here?'

'The doctor asked me to leave.'

MacLeod pushed the constable to one side and rushed into the room, he saw a white clad figure bending over the bed, she had a syringe in her hand and was holding it to the drip tube connecting a saline bag to his arm.

MacLeod knocked a trolley at the door

231

as he went in, and the doctor looked up. It was Muriel Lamont. She gasped and picked up a scalpel from a tray beside the bed. She held it at the Galloping Major's throat.

'Stop, let me leave or I will kill him.'

'Don't be stupid, Doctor, you are caught, you can't get away, now put the knife down and come with me.'

Doctor Muriel Lamont only thought about it for a second, she had picked up the scalpel as a reflex action, she put it down, 'That was a stupid thing to do, I have been rather silly, I shouldn't have come here.'

Milton walked forward and got hold of her arm, he saw a look of resignation on her face and felt she would be amenable to going with him. Cleary held her other arm and they propelled her out of the door, quickly and quietly without fuss. 'We'll take her to the office,' said Cleary. As he left he pressed an alarm button to get the attention of a nurse.

MacLeod went to the old tramp's bed. He saw an old man, with a trim beard, he had been cleaned up and now appeared to be what he was, a retired Army officer, his eyes were closed, he opened his eyes and looked round.

'Has she gone, my word that was a close thing.'

He looked up and said to MacLeod, 'Are you the police, I do hope so. Mean and poor though my life is, I would rather keep it if you don't mind.'

'Have you seen the doctor before?'

'Of course I've seen her before, she gave me that rotten bottle of whiskey, my stomach must be getting soft.'

'Before that, think man.'

'No, I don't think so, I have never seen her before.'

At that a nurse came into the room, MacLeod told her what had happened and she checked the drip. She pulled the curtain round his bed.

'Nothing wrong here, it's a good job you came in, an air bubble in this could have been serious in fact it may have been fatal.'

MacLeod wished she had whispered, but like the whole of the medical profession, once the curtains are round the patient's bed they think they are deaf. From his brief encounter with this lonely old tramp, he quite liked him.

MacLeod left the room and was walking down the corridor thought of something and turned to the lack lustre constable.

'Constable, if you ever leave your post again, you won't have a post to leave, now get back in there and look after him, do your job.'

The young officer stood up to attention. He had been in the force long enough to know if he had proffered any excuse it would not have done him any good, in fact may have set MacLeod off again.

He accepted the rebuke in silence. A shaken disturbed and resentful young constable returned to the room, how was he to know all the doctors in the hospital? He did as he was told by doctors. He had learned something by this mistake, he would never regard symbols of authority i.e. white coats as sacrosanct again.

MacLeod went to the office and found the door locked, he knocked and was confused, no reply. He was about to retrace his steps when a panting Constable Cleary arrived.

'She got away, that woman can run. She knew the hospital better than I did. I've put out a call for assistance, they should be here in a couple of minutes.'

'How on earth did she get away from both of you?'

'She seemed so quiet we weren't holding on to her and she suddenly shrugged us off and ran, we couldn't catch her. Your DS is fitter than me so I stopped to call for assistance to cover the exits. I knew you would come back here, I came to tell you. I haven't seen the DS since, I hoped he had got her.'

MacLeod was concerned, John Milton was fit, but not that fit, he would be back soon. They were soon joined by the local Inspector and a systematic search of the hospital grounds was commenced. Constable Cleary told the hospital administrator exactly what was going on, he found it easier to keep him informed of everything, after all he could help in many ways.

After half an hour MacLeod was becoming concerned, John Milton had not returned, he was hoping that he had not hurt himself in the chase. As he was about to go out and search himself a dishevelled and dirty Milton walked through the door.

'That bitch, I followed her to the basement and she ran like a hare. I followed her round a corner into a room only she wasn't there, she was behind the open door and slammed it shut on me and locked it.

Next time I go anywhere I want a radio, I was in some sort of store room, I climbed up to a window but I slipped and fell, the flaming boxes fell on top of me. It's a good job they heard me shouting or I could have been there forever.'

Despite the situation, MacLeod had to stifle his mirth. John Milton was fastidious in his dress and habits. His idea of casual clothing was a blazer and tie with grey trousers. Only once had MacLeod seen him in denim jeans and they had a knife-edged crease in them. He wished he had a camera.

'I think she has got away. Ring the office, John Lamont has to be brought in now in case she rings him, we don't want both of them to get away.'

Milton felt better having something to do, but his pride was really hurt, this woman was both fit and a very good actress, he was convinced she was going to come quietly. Then she exploded into life, she jumped so fast he didn't have time to stop her, and he had tried to catch her, he thought he had her a couple of times but she seemed to melt from his grip.

When she closed the door on him, he heard her laugh. She was leading him to that place. She really knew the hospital well. She obviously had spent some considerable time in the place. He was not surprised to hear later that she had spent two years as junior doctor at the Southern General after qualifying.

★ ★ ★

Reade got the phone call from Milton and shouted to Janet MacBain, 'Muriel

Lamont has got away, she tried to kill the Galloping Major, we've got to bring in her husband — now.'

'MacDonald, you interviewed him the first time, didn't you?'

'Yes.'

'Get your coat we'll go and get him, make sure I don't get the wrong man.'

They hurried out, and ran downstairs to the car, MacDonald drove to Innellan as fast as he could under the circumstances. The road is winding and with the sea on one side and the houses on the other, he was careful but did break the speed limit on one or two occasions.

They arrived at Innellan and drove up the steep hill past the church, at the top of the hill they turned right into a wooded copse, the drive to the big house stretched before them. As they came out of the wood, the tyres crunched on the pebbles which covered the drive. The big house stood solidly before them, three levels with double and triple bay windows overlooking the village and the Clyde towards the Ayrshire Coast.

The house and gardens were well

looked after. Neither Janet nor Rod were thinking about the house, views or how much a place like this might cost to upkeep. They were concentrating on their quarry.

MacDonald stopped at the side entrance to the house and he and MacBain nearly fell out of the car, they ran round the back of the house, where they saw a one storey building, tastefully built to blend in with the main house, the door was open and inside was clean and sharp with the smell of disinfectant so characteristic of the medical profession.

The receptionist stood up and tried to stop them going into a room at the end of the corridor. MacBain merely thrust her warrant card in the girl's face and kept going.

They burst open the door, and saw John Lamont standing at his desk, he was holding the telephone in his hand, he was leaning on his arm on the desk.

He looked as if he was about to faint. He looked at both officers with deep blue eyes, tears welled up in them. MacBain grabbed the phone and heard the deep whirr of the dialling tone, no one was on the line.

'She's gone.'

MacDonald said 'Was that your wife on the phone?'

'Yes.'

Lamont was distressed and he seemed about to faint, MacDonald pulled a chair to him and made him sit down.

'Where is she?'

'I don't know, she didn't say, but she isn't coming back.'

MacBain said 'Get your coat, you are coming with us.'

19

John Lamont sat in the interview room at Dunoon Police Station, he mulled over the last hour, he was holding the telephone when the door of his office was thrown open and two police officers rushed in.

He was in shock, they were asking about his wife, where was she, what did she say. He didn't know what to say, he couldn't think properly, he needed Muriel but she wasn't there.

They asked him to go with them and he went; he was led to the police car, as if he were a child.

As they were leading him out of the office he remembered his children and asked Fran, the receptionist, to look after them for a while until he came back, he wouldn't be long.

He had looked at the officers for confirmation but they didn't look him in the eye. He was more confused than ever,

241

what was going on, he couldn't take it all in.

He felt he should ask them why he was going with them but his mind was numb. He didn't have the energy and he couldn't get the telephone call from Muriel out of his mind, it filled him totally. The last thing she had said was that she loved him and the boys and to give them a hug from her.

MacLeod found John Lamont in this state when he returned to the station. He saw a big man, over six foot tall, his hair was blonde receding slightly. He was well built, but was developing a paunch. He looked fit and healthy. MacLeod was sure this was not the shadow he had seen at the window of Hamilton's room.

Lamont looked up at MacLeod, he had tears welling up in his eyes. 'She's left me and I don't know why.'

He said it with such pain in his voice that he felt for the man, he then shook himself and thought that he should not feel sympathy for this man, he was a murder suspect and any sign of sympathy on his part could ruin the clinical interview he had to perform.

MacBain followed MacLeod into the room, under normal circumstances Detective Sergeant Milton would have accompanied him, but MacBain had brought this man in and MacLeod felt she should be at the final interview.

Another very good reason for having Janet with him was his instinct. He had listened intently to the description from the officers exactly how Lamont appeared when he was brought to the station; he felt Lamont would be more open with a woman present.

MacBain put on the tape recorder and after the loud beep introduced herself for the tape purposes, and MacLeod said who he was and asked John Lamont to introduce himself. He told Lamont that the interview was being taped.

'John, do you know why you are here?'

'No, my wife told me she was leaving and not coming back.'

'I would like to put some questions to you about your whereabouts on certain dates, and whether your wife was with you at the time.'

MacLeod sat down at the desk, put a file in front of him and the interview began in earnest.

* * *

In the Southern General Hospital, life went on as normal. The flurry of excitement when the hospital was searched had died down and the serious business of healing the sick resumed.

Down in the basement Doctor Muriel Lamont had hidden herself amongst the dusty filing cabinets and had eluded the searchers. She picked up a file and walked briskly out of the basement. She walked up the stairs and passed two police officers leaning on a desk talking to a receptionist. She felt a surge of fear as she walked past, small beads of sweat on her brow, and she went to the public telephone in reception. She was passed by three other officers, who merely glanced at her whilst she made a hurried and distasteful call to her husband.

She briskly walked back down the stairs back to the basement, she forced herself not to run and give the game away.

Muriel knew this hospital well, at the back of the cabinets where she replaced the files, there was a small and unused room. The door was always locked, but she had acquired a key when she was a very junior hospital doctor. She had lived in residence then and the need to be alone was sometimes unbearable.

She thought about her hidey-hole, she had been searching for a file in the cabinet room, computers were just being introduced, but she needed an old file and had been given the keys and directions and that was it. Whilst poring over the files she found an odd key on the key ring, it took her some time to find the right lock, no flimsy Yale lock this, a solid mortise, from its appearance it hadn't been used for years. She found the door and with a little effort opened it.

The sight that greeted her was of a small office, covered in cobwebs and dust. In one corner was a small gas fire, she had fiddled about with it and managed to get it working whilst she worked at the hospital.

She didn't hand the key in when she went back to the main office, no security staff in those days, a happier and freer age before the dark cloud of criminal activity had descended on hospitals. She kept the key on her keyring as a talisman when she left the hospital. She never expected to ever use the key again.

She looked at the floor, it was dusty but had been disturbed by tramping feet of the policemen who had made a search of the filing room. She smiled at the loud tramping of their feet, they did not see her slip into the shadows. One had passed within touching distance of her but had missed her.

She had discarded her white coat at the exit of the basement, they would think she had left the hospital, and they were called from the search of the basement when it was found.

She went to 'her' door, she put the key in the lock and with a little effort the key turned. The door opened inwards, no Heath and Safety legislation when this room was built. The door creaked a little as it opened, although she knew that no one was left to hear, she looked over her shoulder, fear gripped her heart.

She carefully opened the door and closed it behind her, her face contorted as she closed it gently. She locked the door and let out a deep sigh. It was completely dark, she felt her way to the desk and switched on an old desk lamp. She was delighted to see it lit, electricity had not been cut off. She knew that this light would not pass under the door, she had checked years ago but just in case she found an old coat and put it to the foot of the door.

Muriel sat down, she was exhausted, she had to write a confession and explain everything. She was no fool and knew the police would be seeing her husband now. She also knew that he had nothing to do with everything she had done and he had an alibi every time she had committed murder.

There, she had said it, murder, she felt some remorse for Sister Jenny but not the rest, they deserved it.

She tried to work out when it had all started. She had been a lonely child, she had spent a lot of her time walking in the hills behind Dunoon. She had first seen death when a fisherman had pulled out a wriggling fish from the reservoir in the Bishops Glen, she watched fascinated as he expertly hit the fish with a stone and it stopped wriggling and died.

She wanted to do that, she wanted to know what it felt like. Muriel set up traps for mice, rats, voles and once she got an otter. She didn't think she was torturing the unfortunate animals, but she discovered that if she cut their throats the blood spurted a considerable distance.

All of the animals struggled, but she could inflict a death wound before they turned on her, they would run for a while then drop, their life blood draining into the earth. She watched as their eyes glazed over and they died. They all fought for life.

She was caught by her mother one day at the back step, fortunately the mouse had already died, and she was cutting the still warm body open to look at the steaming insides.

Her mother screamed and her father

came out to see what was wrong. When he saw the scene he merely commented that he was obviously going to have a doctor in the family.

He spoke to her severely and told her that doing that sort of thing when her mother was about was not a lady-like thing to do. He suggested she take over the shed at the bottom of the garden as a sort of laboratory and from then on she was able to conduct her experiments in private.

She worked hard at her school work and became a doctor. She never lost her fascination for blood.

When the bulldozers had moved in at the back of her lovely home in Windie-sham, she thought about her aunt and the house in Scotland. She laid her plans well, took two days off work and told her husband she was working overnight because there was a critical experiment.

She knew he wouldn't ring her, he never did. He was a Freemason and was going to one of his dinners, they had a babysitter for the night. No finger of suspicion could be pointed to him. It was bad luck she got a speeding ticket on the M74, she thought about giving a false name but that would make the police suspicious, she hoped they would not connect the ticket with her visit.

She got into the house easily enough, no one locked doors in this area. She crept upstairs and her aunt was fast asleep, she had an empty syringe in her hand, as she pushed the lethal dose of air into her aunt's neck, she stirred.

Muriel was good, it would feel like a midgie bite and afterwards would look like one in the hair line. She watched as her aunt died. There was no struggle, her breathing just stopped.

She got out the way she came and walked through the woods back to her car. The irony was that she took the same route as Mary on the way to meet her lover. Muriel drove back home, she had not used the ferry to get to Innellan, she didn't want to be connected to this area, it was a lot further to drive but safer.

She arrived back home, completely exhausted and went to bed, her husband had rather a lot to drink the night before and did not notice her get into bed.

A few hours later the local police arrived and told them that her aunt had been found dead, her tiredness dissipated, they were free. She was glad she had got back. They took statements from them as to their whereabouts the night before. Someone suspected, but it was put down as natural causes and they inherited the lot.

Muriel remembered the day she met the Duchess. She had been asked to do the surgery at Tramps Hall in Glasgow, she nearly missed her. The Duchess came in late, she had a small wound on her arm and the nurse had just left. Muriel decided to dress the wound, as she was doing so the Duchess began to talk, probably because Muriel was a new face to her, she rambled on about her children and how someone had kidnapped them.

Muriel was a little bored with her ramblings, but she froze when she started talking about her rich family in Innellan, how they had been so cruel to her and had thrown her out. She took a long look at Mary, but saw nothing she could recognise.

As the Duchess was about to leave she asked for her name 'for record purposes'. Mary Bland was the reply. As an aside, with beating heart, she asked for her maiden name.

Mary said she had no other. Mary had a small vestige of pride and didn't want her family name sullied by her present circumstances.

After everyone had left, Muriel got into conversation with Sister Jenny. As a doctor, Muriel was adept in getting people to talk without realising that she was after information.

Sister Jenny gave Muriel everything she wanted, or rather didn't want to know. On her way home she began to plan Mary's death. She had seen little of Mary in their youth, but she remembered her as a spoilt little madam.

She had a tendency to nip Muriel, pull her hair and when Muriel retaliated Mary would run crying to her father and Muriel would get into trouble. No, Muriel did not like Mary.

Muriel spent as much time as she could in the area of Tramps Hall, she had a set of rough clothing and dressed down enough to fit in with the tramps. Her husband thought she was either working or out on calls, he was easy to dupe, he was so trusting.

She found Mary's routine and where she was always alone, Muriel chose her place well. Glasgow Central Railway Station was dangerous but Mary always went to the Ladies when she had enough money and got a shower. The attendants didn't like it but Mary needed to be clean and she didn't cause any trouble.

Once she had found her routine Muriel dressed as herself and met her, 'accidentally' in the toilets. She asked about her arm, a natural thing for her to do as a doctor and in passing told her that she thought she knew who she was.

Mary froze at this and was about to run away when Muriel said that she had been looking for her children for her, but had discovered her mother had died and her father wanted to see her again. Muriel told Mary not to tell anyone and she would make arrangements to meet her again the following night, she gave Mary some money to get some decent clothes.

It was unfortunate that Mary decided to spend the money on alcohol and didn't keep her mouth shut. Muriel picked her up at the station, she had seen the Galloping Major following Mary, but Muriel kept her head low as Mary lurched into the car.

She called her by name and Mary got in the car. Mary had been contrite at not buying the clothes, as all alcoholics are when caught out in a lie. Muriel was a little upset, but she gave her a bottle of whiskey to 'keep her warm' as they were going to drive round to Innellan. Mary guzzled the whiskey with gusto. Muriel had beefed up the whiskey with some pure alcohol, which soon made Mary dizzy and she lapsed into unconsciousness.

Muriel drove round to Dunoon the long way round, as she approached Whistiefield junction she turned left to take the twisting route to Ardentinny. As she came to the high point overlooking the loch, the horizon was lit up by Coulport Naval Base, it looked like a small town in the dark night.

The lights lit up the car and she looked at Mary slumped in the passenger seat, she had her mouth open, saliva was dribbling from the left side. Muriel was disgusted, *this thing* would take everything from her if she were discovered.

Muriel pulled over into the cove she had selected. It was quiet, no one was about, she pulled Mary from the car, and lay her on the ground.

The tide would soon take her out to sea, never to be seen again. She was about to get into the car when an urge came over her, inexplicable and urgent, she gave in to it.

She got a scalpel from her bag and cut Mary's throat and watched the blood spurt. An anger came over her, she began to stab the body in a frenzy, all the youthful rage pent up inside her finally spent.

It was irrational but she felt much better, she was gasping for breath when she stood up. She looked down at her clothes, damn, she was covered in blood.

She went to the loch and cleaned as much as she could off herself. She looked round, and could not see anyone. She went home, changed in the laboratory and incinerated her clothes.

Muriel suddenly felt cold, she resisted the impulse to try out the gas fire, she didn't want to draw attention to her little room. She thought about Sister Jenny, she had some regret about her. But somehow she couldn't control herself, Sister Jenny was awake and looking at her with pity in her eyes and she had to approach her from the back.

Sister Jenny didn't try to defend herself when she lunged and cut her throat, just at the right spot, her trusty scalpel struck home unerringly with a mind of its own. Sister Jenny didn't even try to stem the flow and she died quietly and with a dignity Muriel found deeply disturbing.

Sister Jenny knew what was happening, and she gave herself up to her God with a sigh. Muriel had never thought about the afterlife, whatever happened she was definitely going to another place far away from Sister Jenny.

When Muriel had overheard that the Detective Superintendent was born on the same day as the Duchess' first born, she was convinced that he was her son, he had the same colouring and his build was similar to her uncle, he would have to go.

She knew the Argyll Hotel very well, she had suggested to the receptionist that the rooms at the front were the best rooms in the house and it would be good for business, the girl had taken it in without question.

When she went round later and looked at the register when no one was about she was pleased when she saw where her quarry lay. She had dressed in black at the surgery in Church Street, and slipped up the fire escape.

Hamilton had obligingly lay with his neck exposed, a sharp slash and he was spurting blood, she had been slow, she had watched the blood spurt and enjoyed the sight. He had fought for his life, and she was about to give him the death blow when that meddlesome nosy parker MacLeod had crashed through the door.

She had nearly been caught.

She had rushed the few streets back to the Surgery and changed into clean clothes. She had slipped away from her post at Dunoon Hospital, and got back before anyone realised. Luck was on her side.

When Hamilton came in she had done her utmost to save his life. She had the time later to see to him, she was a well known visitor to the Inverclyde. Muriel regretted this loose end, she considered trying to get to him but it was too dangerous. She would definitely be caught and she had no intention of standing trial.

The Galloping Major was easy, he was always hanging round the railway station. She gave him a bottle of whiskey and she followed him to the underpass near Harry Ramsden's, she waited until he had drunk sufficiently to make him comatose and was about to approach him in this quiet spot when a young couple came past.

They were meddlesome and saw that he was ill, so they called an ambulance, drat these mobile phones. She had to get rid of him, he may recognise her as the person who picked Mary up that fateful night.

Well, she nearly had him, an air bubble in his saline drip, she would have had him too if it hadn't been for that man again MacLeod, she should have killed him instead of Hamilton that night.

Muriel went into the drawer and found some old paper, she was delighted to see that one piece still had her youthful script clearly showing, this was before her handwriting deteriorated into the doctor's scrawl.

She took a pen from her pocket and carefully wrote her confession. She wanted to make sure that her husband would never be blamed for her actions. She felt a pang in her heart when she remembered his bewildered reaction when she told him she was leaving him and would not be back, he would know by now what she had done, she hoped he wouldn't hate her.

Muriel knew her boys would be distraught at her disappearance, she loved all of them so much, she felt a lump in her throat, but after all she was only doing what the lioness does in the wild, providing for and protecting her family.

The strenuous actions of the day and the dim light of the soft light on the desk made her so tired. She finished writing and looked down. She folded the papers and searched for an envelope but couldn't find one. She wrote in large capitals, DETECTIVE CHIEF INSPECTOR MACLEOD.

She put her head on her arms on the desk and went to sleep.

20

MacLeod and MacBain returned to the incident room, they were exhausted. The interview had gone well, but not entirely to plan. Lamont had been open and, it appeared, honest with them. He had provided alibi's for every murder except for the attack on Hamilton. He could only say that he was at home with his children.

The rest of the team were patiently waiting for the result. MacLeod wasted no time, 'I don't believe he committed the murders, and I know he didn't attack Mr Hamilton, I saw the outline and it certainly wasn't him.'

Janet MacBain was not so certain, 'He could have been with his wife, he could have been with her.'

Reade was a little bemused. 'I thought we had him, what happened?'

'He came over as a genuinely upset man,' said MacLeod, 'but we need to check his alibis. I'll have to see the Fiscal to get a remand until they are checked out.'

Reade looked at a notepad on his desk, 'Will you call a Constable Cleary at the Southern General, he wants to speak to you personally.'

MacLeod was feeling and looking deflated, the events of the day were beginning to tell. He went into his office, he was now almost sure that Lamont was not guilty. He turned to MacBain, 'Get those alibis checked.'

He walked into his office and rang Constable Cleary. 'Right what is it, something important I hope.'

'Yes, we've found her car. It was parked at the back of the neurological depart-ment. Before you say anything, this is a big place and it took some time to find it. Sorry about it being so long. What do you want us to do?'

MacLeod thought for a moment, 'Have you isolated it?'

'Yes, but we didn't want to take it away until you gave the word, sir.'

'Good, keep watch in case she returns for it.'

MacLeod put the phone down, he called towards the main office, 'John, could you get in here? I need you.'

Detective Sergeant Milton came into the office and shut the door behind him; when MacLeod wanted to talk it was usually a private meeting. 'They've found her car in the hospital, don't you think it's unusual? Do you think she is the kind of person to go without it?'

'I don't know, perhaps she legged it on foot.'

'No, I don't think so, someone else, perhaps. I got the impression she liked her comfort. I've got them keeping observations on the car in case she comes back to it.'

'If she was going to come back to the car, she would have done it by now, she's had plenty of time, it's been over four hours since she got away.'

Milton grimaced, he still remembered the humiliation of being trapped in the dark room in the basement of the hospital.

'On the other hand,' Milton went on, 'perhaps she is waiting until the middle of the night to get to her car.'

'My thoughts too, did the search team check all the rooms in the basement?'

'I don't know, maybe they didn't.'

MacLeod was suddenly more alert, the tiredness of a few moments ago was completely dissipated. He began a flurry of activity in the incident room. Reade was instructed to organise a thorough search of the hospital, department by department, room by room, particular attention was to be paid to the basements, no locked door was to be ignored.

MacBain and Lampart were to go to the Lamont's home, a search to be carried out for anything of evidential value.

Morris and MacPherson were urgently required to check John Lamont's alibis, by telephone. If they found witnesses, they were to get the local police to get statements as soon as possible.

'What about the remand?' MacBain asked.

'The Fiscal will do it, tell him, I can't speak at the moment, Detective Sergeant

Milton and I are going to the Southern General. I'll see him when we get back.

★ ★ ★

MacLeod and Milton went straight to the Southern General and met up with Chief Inspector Stewart, the Operational Support Unit Commander, at the police office.

'It's costing a fortune for this, you know. Who's going to foot the bill?' moaned Stewart.

MacLeod kept his temper, money, that's all anyone thought about.

'If we find her, then we have solved the attack on Mr Hamilton, I'm sure the chief constable won't object.'

Stewart went into a sullen silence. Privately he thought that the CID regarded all uniformed officers as their private source of manpower, they weren't wanted unless they became useful. He would never admit it, but he disliked CID officers with their certainty and superior air. This could be traced to him performing an attachment to CID and

265

was rejected as not suitable. That hurt and he never forgot the final interview with the DI. He had made a good career in Uniform, but it still rankled.

Constable Cleary came into the room, he looked a little flustered and said to MacLeod, 'Would you come to the administrator's office, the Chief Executive is getting very agitated about the hospital being turned upside down again. I can't get through to him, perhaps you could, sir.'

MacLeod nodded, he and Milton accompanied Cleary to the administration department. They walked through the general office where it seemed a myriad of office workers were busy as ants at their desks, they hardly looked up as the police officers passed.

They had to wait for a few minutes in the personal assistant's office until the administrator was free to see them. They were offered and gratefully accepted a cup of tea, from a white haired and efficient lady of indeterminate years. They sat in silence and when the buzzer on the intercom went off, Cleary nearly spilt his tea in the saucer.

In the administrator's office, Mr Ian Nesbitt, Chief Administrator for the Southern General sat behind a huge and imposing desk. In front of his desk was a large Mahogany conference table with red leather clad matching chairs. They sat at the conference table. As MacLeod sat down, he noted that these chairs were built for comfort, for long and tense meetings. He thought he should mention them to his wife, on second thoughts, perhaps not, he doubted his salary could afford them.

Constable Cleary formally introduced the CID officers, and Nesbitt started the proceedings rather irritably, 'Tell me why my hospital is in uproar again, it isn't good for the staff nor does it help the patients.'

MacLeod had no time to reply when Chief Inspector Stewart appeared at the doorway, 'I thought I had better tell you at once, a body has been found in the basement of this building. A note was with the body for you.'

He handed MacLeod three sheets of

folded paper. His name was clearly marked on the top folded sheet.

MacLeod took the letter and turned to Nesbitt, 'I think that Mr Stewart has replied to your query adequately, I think you will find we will not be bothering you again.'

He put the note in his pocket and as one, MacLeod, Milton and Cleary rose from their seats and left the office.

Nesbitt visibly shrank in his chair, he was a little man with a big ego, he enjoyed the power he had and used it, he was looking forward to showing these officers who was boss in the Hospital, but the news of the body took the wind out of his sails. He knew that MacLeod regarded him with contempt and by his actions showed it. His staff would feel his wrath this afternoon.

On the way out of Nesbitt's office, Stewart told MacLeod that the body was a female and was in a small room in the basement. They had to break into the room as the key had been lost. It appeared from the description that it was his missing doctor. His manner had changed towards MacLeod from their earlier encounter, he was polite and respectful, the resentment had disappeared. MacLeod had earned his respect.

They went to the basement where they looked at the body from the door of the small room where Doctor Muriel Lamont had breathed her last. At the door was a constable, he made a note of who was there and what they did. MacLeod was pleased the Operational Support Unit had been well trained in scene preservation.

There was a small lamp on the desk illuminating her in a small circle of light. She had her head on her hands and looked asleep, except that her lips were blue, her skin was pallid and she was not breathing. She looked like a statue waiting for the make-up artist to come to make her look alive.

The door had been forcefully pushed open, MacLeod looked down and saw at the corner of the door an old piece of rag, he sniffed the air, 'Is that gas?'

The constable at the door answered, 'There's a leak in the gas fire, we've had the gas turned off, it's a good job she didn't light it, it was a small leak but the pathologist that came down to declare her dead said that she died only about an hour ago, she may not have known about the leak and putting the coat to the door stopped the gas dispersing, he is arranging a post-mortem as soon as forensic finish, they haven't arrived yet.'

MacLeod was delighted he didn't have to contact the Fiscal for this area, it was his case in the strict sense inasmuch he had organised the search, but he could happily leave the rest of the paperwork to Stewart.

'Over to you, Mr Stewart, you and your lads seem to have this well in hand. Oh! Just to tidy up everything, could you get the car examined, she may be dead but I want to make sure she did the murders!'

'Always the belt and braces man,' muttered Milton.

'What was that?' MacLeod hadn't quite heard what Milton had said, he was preoccupied for the moment.

'Nothing, I thought we should get back to the office. The rest of the team will want to know.'

'Yes, get the car round the front will you, and will you ring the Fiscal at Dunoon and ask him to be present at the meeting, if he has the time, of course.' Milton left.

'You and your team have done a brilliant job. Thank you.' MacLeod said to Stewart.

Thank you, someone said thank you, Stewart was taken aback, he rarely had been thanked for anything. He swelled with pride and looked at MacLeod, anything this man wants, he gets, he thought.

'It's a pity we didn't start the search earlier, she may have been alive.'

'Don't blame yourself, you got here as soon as you could. After all I didn't call you until I thought about it. If we had done a proper search earlier we may have been able to save her.'

He looked at Muriel and thought this probably was the outcome she hadn't anticipated but perhaps it was best for all concerned, a trial and a conviction would devastate her sons. He had little sympathy for Muriel, but her children were another matter.

He fervently hoped that John Lamont's alibis were upheld, he didn't want more children in the care of the local authority. They deserved more than that. It wasn't their fault, parents rarely chose their children, and the converse is true.

* * *

On the way back to the office, MacLeod read the letter from Muriel to him, he was shocked at her callousness, the only saving grace so far as he was concerned was her obvious concern for her husband and children. He read the letter in silence.

* * *

All the team were present in the incident room, Duncan Grey had not arrived, but was expected soon. There was an air of expectation.

The door crashed open, Duncan Grey

had arrived. He was, as usual, in a rush. As he came through the door, Constable Morris had handed him a cup of coffee. He had really poured it from the coffee machine for himself, but decided the Fiscal needed it more than he did.

'Thank you, son. Am I late? I hope you haven't started yet, Cameron. There was a little problem in the office, but I am free now. All yours.'

Grey settled himself down, and MacLeod began his debrief.

'As you know Muriel Lamont has been found dead, the postmortem is being performed now, but I don't expect any signs of foul play. She left a letter for me and I'll read it to you now.'

He opened the sheets of paper, her handwriting was clear and concise, unusual for a doctor, but she had made an effort to make her handwriting legible, the effort had unconsciously made her writing almost child like.

Dear Cameron,
  I was a little sorry about my Aunt, but she had the means for us to get a

better life, she had had a good life, and all she was doing was to hang on to the house and money. I had to wait until Mary had been officially declared dead and then a year or so. She died peacefully, I injected her with air, she didn't know much about it. The only fly on the ointment was that I got a speeding ticket, but I knew that police forces don't talk to each other much so I was fairly safe.

I had to kill Mary. She would have taken everything away from my family. I did not like her when she was a child, she was selfish and vindictive and I certainly did not expect her to be anything else as an adult.

I met her when I was standing in at the Tramps Hall, she told me she was going to find her family, I recognised her, although she did not recognise me, and I had to kill her. I made a plan, unfortunately it did not come to fruition, first because the tide threw her on shore a day before I expected and second, you were in charge.

If she had come to land a day later,

274

there would have been no enquiry, I would have certified the cause of death as drowning, the stab wounds I would have said were normal for a body being tossed and turned in the sea.

Next, you do not give up. So you can blame yourself for Sister Jenny. I knew you would get to her and had to get rid of her before she could speak to you about me. I took the money from the safe, I should have got rid of it, but I could not. I gave it to charity, I put it in one of those envelopes which are put through the letter box. I won't say which one, you may want to get it back.

I'm sorry about the Superintendent, it was stupid of me, but when I overheard his talking to you I had a strong feeling he was her child and had to get rid of him. I hope he recovers. You nearly caught me then. So close.

I found out about Joe Armstrong when I happened to be in Dunoon and overheard two Americans talking about hiring him to find someone, I got into *his office and took the file, you will find it in my laboratory.'*

MacLeod stopped reading and looked at Janet MacBain, she nodded and held up the file and showed it to the rest of the room. He continued.

'I saw the old tramp when I picked up Mary at the Glasgow Central; I thought he saw me. I was going to get him but two nosy parkers called an ambulance. I was stupid to try to kill him in the hospital but I was desperate. You nearly had me then.

I did everything, my husband knew nothing about it and you will find that he was well away from everything. I did it all.

I'll leave this letter here, sometime soon you will have the hospital searched again. I'm going to disappear and you will not find me.

Tell my beloved husband John that I love him and I adore my sons, but it is best for everyone that I just go and they don't see me again.

*You have caused me all these
problems, so I will make sure your
family will suffer the way mine have. I
will get your wife, and you won't know
the time or the day.*

Muriel Lamont MD

MacLeod shivered as he read the last
paragraph. He looked up and saw the
look of horror on the faces of his team
and Duncan Grey. There was a long
silence, eventually broken by Grey.

'You are sure, aren't you. It was Muriel
Lamont in that room.'

'Yes, I'm sure, In fact after I read the
letter I went to the Mortuary to make
sure. It was her.'

There was a stir in the room, MacLeod
told the team to tidy up the incident
room. Grey got hold of MacLeod's arm,
'Come with me, you need to unwind. The
others can manage. I had John Lamont
released before I came here I knew he had
nothing to do with the murders before
you came back. He's gone home to his
children.'

* * *

MacLeod and Grey went to the Fiscal's office, where Grey produced a bottle of eighteen year old Glenturret Whiskey and a jug of water.

'I have kept this for some time, waiting for a special occasion. I think this is it. Congratulations Cameron, but the threat in that letter is horrific. You and I need to unwind.'

MacLeod and Grey sat in comfortable companionship for a couple of hours. Grey went over the case with MacLeod and then tried to ease MacLeod's mind. When there was only two inches left in the bottle, MacLeod seemed relaxed enough in Grey's mind, he rang MacLeod's wife and told her to collect her husband from the next ferry and he rang the police office and arranged a lift for him.

They finished the bottle. MacLeod should have been well and truly inebriated but he appeared stone cold sober. He was not in the mood to get drunk, he could not get the threat from his mind.

As he was leaning on the side of the boat, he looked towards Holy Loch, he could see the shore line towards Ardentinny. The mountain tops behind were covered in snow, soon summer would melt the snow and they would not stand out so well against the horizon.

He thought about the events of the past week. He had done a good job, or rather his team had, and they would return to their normal and routine duties. After an enquiry like this he wanted to get back to house breakings, domestic assaults, anything except a psychopathic killer. He felt he had been in her mind and he didn't like what he saw, he felt her shadow loomed over his family. It would take some time for the darkness to dissipate.

He was dog tired and held his wife very close when she met him, she was startled at his show of affection in public, she would find out why sometime, but not now. She hoped he could get a good night's sleep before something else came up.

MacLeod was almost asleep before they got home.

Other titles in the
Linford Mystery Library:

THAT INFERNAL TRIANGLE

Mark Ashton

An aeroplane goes down in the notorious Bermuda Triangle and on board is an Englishman recently heavily insured. The suspicious insurance company calls in Dan Felsen, former RAF pilot turned private investigator. Dan soon runs into trouble, which makes him suspect the infernal triangle is being used as a front for a much more sinister reason for the disappearance. His search for clues leads him to the Bahamas, the Caribbean and into a hurricane before he resolves the mystery.

THE GUILTY WITNESSES

John Newton Chance

Jonathan Blake had become involved in finding out just who had stolen a precious statuette. A gang of amateurs had so clever a plot that they had attracted the attention of a group of international spies, who habitually used amateurs as guide dogs to secret places of treasure and other things. Then, of course, the amateurs were disposed of. Jonathan Blake found himself being shot at because the guide dogs had lost their way . . .